Callum

ADDISON JAMES

ADDISON JAMES

To my family, who can never read this book, but whose love and support encouraged me to write it anyway.

CONTENTS

CONTENT NOTES

- Imprisonment

- Physical mutilation (not permanent, due to immortality/regenerative healing)

- Harm that could be analogous to medical experimentation (off page, discussed)

- Not exceptionally graphic eye stuff

- Off page rape of the FMC

- Fighting, including killing of enemies

- 18+ sex scenes

- 18+ language

CHAPTER ONE

CALLUM

The moon, a few days past full, still sets my blood pumping as I bounce on the balls of my feet, waiting for the signal.

Heath rolls his eyes at me. "That desperate for a fight?"

I grin at him, my sharpened incisors on display, a look so feral it would make anyone flinch. Not Heath, though. I never know if it's the sibling thing, or if he's just seen far worse than me. "Always."

He rolls his eyes again, the movement emphasizing the slowness of the left one, the scar cutting through it. He huffs and apparently decides to ignore me, pushing his too-long hair off his face before hefting his sword.

"You're not?" It's been months since we've gotten anything resembling a fight.

"I have better things to think about than fighting," he says. He doesn't mean it to be cutting. He might not even be referring to Chase. But I hear it anyway. There are plenty of unmated wolves in the world, but I don't happen to be related to any of them anymore, and there's no end of reminders.

I turn to my own sword. The sword is less complicated. War is trustworthy, and my sword will do its job.

It's just Heath and me here today. Celia has always had more important things to do than fight the small-scale battles directly, and Bryce and Mae are still celebrating their honeymoon, three and a half years after mating. We see them every few months or so, and then they disappear again. I didn't even think to ask Bryce if he'd want to be here with us today.

But that's okay. This place has come across Celia's desk as the type of cesspit it's our responsibility to wipe out, but they shouldn't be dangerous enough to take more than Heath and me. Honestly, from everything I'm seeing, Heath and I could probably handle it on our own, without the dozen or so armed pack members waiting for me to give the go-order.

Everyone is standing around waiting. Every single member of the pack that's here was hand-selected by me, just as dangerous with their weapons of choice as their teeth and claws. Every single one is fully prepared to separate heads from shoulders tonight, the only way to make sure beings like us really die.

It may be overkill, but after what Celia read, I'm prepared to be a little over-zealous about this.

I crack my neck, turning my head to look at the compound through the trees. It looks like a nice old manor house. Maybe it was, once. But I know the type of magic they do in there, and it makes my stomach churn.

I've softened on magic in the last four hundred or so years—hard not to, with Bryce and Heath mating with magic users—but everything in me still tells me to be cautious. As Mae told us once, there's magic, and then there's magic. It's all different and some of it will fuck you up.

Mae's been pretty cool, for an emo-looking little magic user who wasn't even born within the same millennium as my brother, even if I've barely gotten to know her yet.

"What are we waiting for?" Heath grumbles next to me, shifting impatiently. "I know you're living for the thrill of the hunt, but some of us have people waiting for us back home, Callum."

The low blow lands, and I try not to flinch, but Heath has been my brother for every single one of my thousand years, and he knows he went too far. "I just meant—"

"You just meant you'd rather be with Chase. I get it, Heath." And I do. I don't blame him. I can see it in his eyes, hear it in his voice; the wolf inside him is driving him back to his mate, gnawing at his mind, and this is the result.

I've watched all my siblings fall in love. I've seen them develop these wonderful, eternal bonds, where they'd do anything for their mates, kill and die and live for them. And my siblings-by-fate are some of my favorite people in the world, too.

I don't regret not finding my mate. It'll happen when it happens, I always tell myself.

I hold my sword tighter. And until it does, I have this.

***

I make us wait until the compound has gone quiet, until my enhanced senses don't pick up any more conversation or casual activity.

Perhaps it isn't sporting to hunt prey that might be asleep in their beds. But I'm not sporting, and these people deserve nothing less.

They're a cabal of magic users specializing in enslavement spells. Most of them will be used on humans, although it didn't get brought to our attention until Celia received a report that they'd gotten to some wolves. Only the lowest type of creature would take away another's will.

I can't contemplate the type of magic it must take to do it, but from the way this place feels, it must be damn powerful, and so deeply evil I can't imagine most sane creatures ever touching it.

I growl, flashing sharp incisors even if there's no one to see it. Creatures like that don't deserve honorable deaths. Let them die in their beds.

And if it lessens the chances that they'll have time to work any freaky magic on the rest of us, that they could possibly work an enslavement spell on any of the wolves under my command, then I'll gladly jump on that.

The wolves following me don't need any orders. They all know the score. Kill everything here. If they have any slaves currently under their thrall, free them if it's safe to do so. And find anything they might be using to pull off these rituals. We still don't fully know how they work, and neither Mae nor Chase have been especially helpful.

"Not my brand of magic," Chase had shrugged, and Heath had glared at me for even potentially implying something so unsavory about his mate, so I'd let it drop.

Heath just raises his eyebrows at me when we draw alongside the building, then tilts his head to the left, and I nod. We split there, both making our own way inside.

I force open a window. Not the most subtle approach, but I've never been an especially subtle guy.

As soon as the window breaks, I nearly fall backwards. Some sort of spell is released, and every dark, terrible scent, every trace of magic hidden by the manor's walls comes pouring out at me.

And one scent, sweet and laced with tragedy, the only good note among the rotten rest, finds me.

I growl, and I can feel my sharpening fang dig into my lip. My claws lengthen, and I crouch forward, entering a stance ready to leap, to fight, much more suited to a beast than a man.

But that's practically all I am right now. A beast, because somewhere in there, somewhere in this death-scented hellhole, is mine. And they've been waiting for me to find them, needing me to find them.

Mindless of my surroundings, mindless of what might be waiting on the other side, I oblige, going headfirst through the window, ready to slaughter anything in the path to my mate.

CHAPTER TWO

CALLUM

Wolves are built to protect our mates. We have razor-sharp claws and teeth strong enough to break a femur. We're stronger, faster, smarter. And we all train with weapons practically from birth.

I'm more capable than most. I've been a warrior since the day I was born, lived on the battlefield, and honed my skills against the best in the world. But none of that prepared me for today, when my wolfish instincts set all my senses to a preternatural focus, until the only thought is finding them.

We haven't been subtle, and the enemy is no longer in their beds. I know some of them put up a fight, but I cut them down with both sword and claws, tearing through necks. I don't give them time to work spells, eliminating each obstacle like an annoying fly.

We came here with a mission about freeing slaves and finding their secrets, but I ignore it, following only the scent.

I come to a stop in front of a large door, steel and bolted, out of place with the old-style architecture of the rest of the house. The scent continues beyond it, tantalizingly seeping out under the door, and I study it for a brief moment.

I take a running start and break the door down with my shoulders, only stopping for a moment to appraise the damage I'd done. I've heard of wolves being able to force their body to do practically anything when their mate is in danger, but going through a steel door like it's tissue paper seems ludicrous.

The smell is stronger here, and I can't think about anything else.

The space is nearly pitch black, but it's no match for my senses. There's a figure on the floor, and I immediately move, crouching down.

The figure is a woman. She's lying face down on the floor, her hands splayed, and my heart jumps up into my throat. If I couldn't hear her pulse—faint as it is—I would fear she was dead.

But she's alive. Barely, but alive.

She's also barely clothed, a small dress that seems to have seen far better days, maybe a decade or so ago, exposing most of her back from where it's torn. Her arms and legs are essentially bare. So are her feet.

It's cold in here. And if I can feel the cold, she's no doubt freezing.

I look back down at her bare feet—so small, so achingly small, and some stupid part of my brain tells me I should hold one of them, warm it in my large palms—and that's when I realize that there's some sort of chain wrapped around her ankle.

A shackle.

I go cold inside, everything in me seeming to slow and freeze. A shackle. On my mate, on her delicate-looking ankle. Probably cutting into her skin.

I don't dare to rip at the shackle; I won't risk hurting her. But I can at least handle the chain.

Gripping the chain right below her ankle to hold it still, I jerk my other hand sharply, putting all my strength into ripping it. It doesn't move.

I frown. I went through a steel door for my mate just minutes ago, and now I can't break a length of chain?

With a roar, I try again, putting all my strength into it, and at last it snaps.

The foot right above my hand twitches, and I freeze, turning to watch her as she wakes up. She twitches once, twice, then goes still. Like she's playing dead or something, but I can hear her pulse. It's accelerating, picking up, like she's afraid.

Of course she would be. She's been chained up in the pitch black, practically naked, cold and alone, for who knows how long.

"It's okay," I tell her, and my voice is so low and raspy I almost don't recognize it as my own. There's more beast than man in that tone now. I swallow, trying to regulate it, even as I know it's a hopeless act. "It's okay. I won't hurt you." I won't allow anyone to hurt her ever again.

Just the thought sends something coursing through me, something sharp and right. Like every battle, every day training, every choice of my entire life was meant to lead-up to this. Like I've finally found my purpose in life. Like it's all worth it now. Her. Protect her.

My life might have just started making sense, but she seems even more scared, her breaths growing faster, and her muscles twitch, like she's trying to curl up on herself but can't quite force her body to work. "Who... who's there?"

I can't resist the urge to actually touch her any longer. I force my claws to retract, needing to comfort her more than I need to fight right this minute. Running what I hope is a soothing hand down her bare back, I roll her slightly until I can scoop her into my arms. "My name's Callum. And I'm here to rescue you."

It sounds like she stops breathing for a minute. "Rescue?" she asks after a long pause.

"Yeah. You do want to be rescued, right?" I ask, but the question is rhetorical. How could she want to stay here?

Anyway, I know my team and I know my brother. Even if I'd essentially ignored most of the fight, they'd take care of it. This place would be nothing but ash soon enough, and she couldn't stay even if she wanted to.

She doesn't say anything, but a hand shoots out to grab at my shoulder, as if to steady herself. I still, letting her touch me, feeling my heart pound as my mate touches me for the very first time. I wonder if she can feel my heart where she's pressed against my chest.

I hope she can. She should know it beats for her. Will always beat for her.

"How'd you break the chain?" she asks, and her voice sounds faint, like it'll fade away.

Do I tell her wolves can do practically anything for their mates? Do I tell her she's my mate when I don't even know her name yet?

"I'm strong," I tell her, and then I heft her a little closer. Maybe I can give her some warmth from my hold. She's so small against me.

Wolves are rarely small, and I'm bigger than most. I've never really thought about it before, but now I can't help but notice. I'm big, so much bigger than her. All the better to protect her with.

All the better to scare her with. Something sours in me at the thought.

"I won't let anything else hurt you," I tell her.

She doesn't seem to hear me. "That chain was enchanted," she says. "I've tried to break it a thousand times, I should know how good the enchantment is."

She might not look strong, but looks aren't always an accurate indicator of strength for creatures like us. "I'm very strong," I say again, too busy thinking about the thousand times my mate has had to try to free herself from her captors.

Where have I been? What have I been doing, when I should have been here, protecting her?

Her hand hasn't left my shoulder, but it tightens, and I feel little claws dig into my skin. They don't break the skin, and they don't even feel slightly uncomfortable. Honestly, I wish she'd dig deeper. Latch herself to me.

She turns her face to me and I avidly look down at her, taking it in for the first time, the face that's been a mystery in my dreams for a thousand years.

Her soft, plush mouth trembles slightly. Probably fear still, and my heart aches at not being able to soothe it. I look over her nose, small and pointy at the end, then up to her eyes.

My chest seizes. Where her eyes should be are two bloody wounds. The blood is fresh enough that it drips down her cheeks, across her temples.

"What happened?" I demand, grabbing her tighter, as if there's an active threat in this room that I can protect her from.

She sniffs, turning her head slightly, although I can still see the gaping wounds. "It's nothing. I—they always do this."

"Always?" What could that mean? What does she mean, always? How often has she been hurt like this?

For creatures like us—whatever she is—to take damage this severe, something awful must have occurred. It had taken a literal cursed blade from hell for Heath to have his eye damaged permanently.

"Every night," she whispers. "And every morning. They'll come back."

My instincts have never been torn before, not in my entire life. I'm a warrior and I protect my pack. It's been simple. But now I'm torn between curling around her and keeping everything away from her, and going deeper into this manor of horrors to find the fucks who did this to her and feed them their own entrails.

And rip their throats out with my teeth and lay them at her feet. I'd heard Heath say that to Chase once. He'd been absolutely serious at the time, and I'd rolled my eyes at the ridiculousness. But now it makes perfect sense.

There's a noise in the hallway that stops all my thoughts, and I growl and turn away from the door. I'd never turn my back to the enemy, but this puts my body between them and her, and that's the only priority right now.

There's a scuffle of a boot on the floor, and the tension eases slightly. Heath.

"What the fuck, Callum?" he growls, and the woman in my arms tenses.

I rush to soothe her, rubbing my thumb over her shoulder and rumbling out reassurances. "It's just my brother. He's safe, I promise."

Heath has stopped at the door, clearly aware of what's happened, of the precious gift I'm holding in my arms. "It smells like death in here," he says sourly.

I sniff, frowning, but yes, beyond the all-consuming scent of mate and mine—still marred by her fear and her pain, but the delicious, perfect scent under that almost makes everything alright—is the scent of death.

Heath, ignoring my warning growl, strides into the room, then goes over to the shelves I've ignored in favor of going straight to my mate. "What the fuck?" he asks, studying what seems to be jars.

The woman in my arms tenses even further. "They store what they cut from me in here."

Heath's growl almost matches mine, but I ignore him in favor of focusing on my mate, even if she can't see my intense stare. "They cut from you?"

She shrugs, as if it's not a big deal, as if I won't kill every single one of them painfully, slowly, over the course of a thousand years, for it. "It's why they kept me. Good ingredients, they said."

Heath snarls, knocking a dozen glass jars to the ground with one sweep of his arm. He turns to us, his face twisted and feral, but I don't fear it. No, his eyes lock on my mate, the brotherly protectiveness of a sibling-by-fate already coloring his expression. "We'll start the fire here," he says. "Burn it all."

I nod. "That okay with you?" I ask her. It's all going to burn anyway, but I suppose it's her body that's been stored in little jars on a shelf, so she should have a say in how it's handled.

"I... sure?" She doesn't sound very sure, but it has to burn and the sooner I get her out of here, the better. So I nod to Heath, and, trusting him to take care of it, I walk out of the room.

She stills, then sniffs deeply. "It..."

It doesn't smell much better out here than it did in her little room, but I suppose anything would be a marked improvement after that. "It'll only get better from here," I promise her lowly, trying to remember where the nearest door would be. "Let's get you out of here. I think it's about time."

I look down at her as I walk, taking in the details that were obscured in the dark room. Like the red hair, long and tangled around her face. Or the scattering of freckles on her nose and cheekbones.

"What's your name, beautiful?" I ask her, turning down yet another twisting hallway, sure there must be a door at the end of this one.

"Marielle." Her voice is so quiet even I have to strain to hear it.

"Beautiful name," I say, meaning it. Marielle. I want to say it every moment for the rest of my very long life. I want to whisper it against her skin, against her lips, shout it, moan it. I want to say it when she makes me laugh and even when she makes me angry. Always, always. Marielle.

CHAPTER THREE

MARIELLE

I cling to the man holding me tighter as we move.

Move. I'm moving, for the first time in I don't know how many years. I tried to keep track at first, but it's hopeless. I couldn't see. There were no meals to track time by. They didn't need me at regular intervals.

I've long since lost count, and now this man—Callum—is apparently rescuing me.

I wish I could see him. I wish I could do more than just feel this man. All I know about him is his deep voice, his large body, and the warmth from his skin. The way he growls sometimes when he talks. What is he? What is he doing here?

Could he work with them? Maybe he's one of them, but had a change of heart.

I swallow. Or maybe they just pissed him off, and he's taking away a valuable asset of theirs.

Once upon a time, I could have fought to defend myself. I could have at the very least given myself time to run away, even if it was a fight I couldn't win.

But that was years ago. That was before I realized just how vulnerable, how breakable, I can truly be.

Callum's grip on me shifts, and I wince, but all he does is hold me with one arm so he can use his other.

After a moment, I realize he's just opening a door. A door. A door to the outside. It must be. I can smell it, can feel it, calling to me.

I'd nearly forgotten how it smells, the beautiful world out there. But now it comes rushing back, something waiting in the back of my mind for me to be ready for it again.

I hold my breath, waiting to see what Callum does with me. But he doesn't even hesitate, just steps out the door, bringing me back to the outside world.

CHAPTER FOUR

CALLUM

Some of my guards linger around the grounds, but all of them are too smart to try to approach me. I ignore them entirely, instead looking only at her as the moonlight illuminates her face.

She sniffs once, and I think I see some of the tension in her face relax.

There are cars parked somewhere, a dozen or so miles away. I can carry her that far, but I don't like the thought. Not when she's vulnerable and blind and must be scared and cold.

Remembering that fact, I sink to my knees under a big ornamental old tree, laying her carefully in the grass as I hastily strip off my jacket for her. When I turn to give it to her, her hands have sunk into the grass and dirt, tiny claws grasping the earth as if she'll never let it go.

There's a look on her face, something ethereal, something so thin I'm afraid it'll snap with the slightest twitch. I hold my breath.

A tear slips from the corner of her mangled eye. "I haven't felt the earth beneath me in so long," she whispers.

Something moves, and I flinch, realizing I left my sword behind like a fool. I bare my teeth and claws, ready to fight whatever it is.

Something long and snake-like reaches for her, appearing right out of the ground, and I snarl and lunge for it, but she turns her own wrist so she's holding it, and I stop short.

A tree root. A tree root emerges from the earth, wrapping gently around her wrist as she grasps it. Then, like her grasp is permission, roots and vines emerge from the ground, latching onto her, covering her nearly head to toe.

I kneel in the dirt, tense, not knowing whether to rip the vines away or let them stay, not liking how they hide my mate from me. But then she sighs, softly, like all the tension in her releases, and I force myself to hold back.

I watch the entire time, barely using my other senses to scan our surroundings. I hope my guard is keeping watch, because I'm useless as a warrior right now, focused entirely on her.

The vines finally retreat, leaving her lying in the grass. But her skin looks healthier, a soft glow coloring her cheeks. And she sits up, blinking.

Her eyes are back. They're big and bright and green, and right now they're watering so much she looks like she's crying. She blinks repeatedly, moving to kneel, and I rush to help her even as she clearly has it under control.

On her knees, Marielle looks up through the tree limbs to the moon above us, staring at it with wonder across her face.

"You a wolf, Marielle?" I ask, hesitant to break the moment.

She blinks. "No. Why?"

"I've never seen anything else look at the moon like that."

She blinks again. "It's just so beautiful," she says, even as she turns towards me.

Her eyes lock onto mine, so bright and green and wide, and everything between us seems to freeze.

CHAPTER FIVE

MARIELLE

I f seeing the moon—my first sight in who-knows how many years—took my breath away, this man is a close second.

Callum. This is Callum. The man who came here and apparently will take me away from all this, for whatever reason.

He smiles at me, the smile crossing his face slow and easy, and it makes his eyes soften. He has sharp incisors and blood on his face, and I know I should feel fear.

I don't. I should. Maybe at this point, I'm immune to fear.

I worried he wanted to use me the same way the others did, cutting pieces off of me for spell ingredients, but something in his smile soothes away that thought. Not even the blood on his face is enough to bring it back.

I want to touch him, to touch the corners of those brown eyes, or his wavy hair, or the bow in that smile. I keep my hands firmly to myself, but I can't quash the thought.

"Oh."

It takes a second to realize that it's me that's said that, that I let that escape.

His smile widens. "Your eyes are healed then?"

I nod, forcing myself to look away from him and back at the moon, then at the world around us. We're under a massive tree, which I already knew from the roots that had shared their life force with me. And the grounds are sprawling, with the woods—full of so much life—calling from a little ways away.

I don't look at the house. I've never actually seen it before, and I don't think I want to. I don't think I need to. The other one mentioned something about burning it. I hope they do.

"It's all just beautiful," I murmur.

He hums in agreement. "They destroyed your eyes every day?"

"Yes."

"For how long?"

I shrug. "Almost as long as I've been there."

"And how long is that?"

The days and years all blurred together. "What year is it?"

An uncomfortable silence settles for a second, and I wonder if he's not going to tell me for some reason, but then he does. "Two thousand and twenty."

I can't quite catch my breath, and I fall forward slightly, just barely catching myself on my hands. Callum lunges forward, his hands on my hips pulling me back, and I freeze. He's behind me, he's grabbing me and pinning me from behind and he's so much stronger than me and—

"Sorry," he murmurs, removing his hands when I'm upright again, but I don't start breathing correctly again. I turn away from the moon to face him, not liking the prickly feeling of having him at my back.

He says he's not letting me stay there. He seems upset at how I've been treated and says he'll burn this place down, and he's covered in blood, presumably their blood. But who's to say he'll be any better than they are, at the end of the day? A smile isn't a promise, and even promises can be broken.

I can't quite make myself accept that, even as I can't shake the discomfort of having him at my back like that.

"How long has it been, Marielle?"

I swallow. "Almost two hundred years."

His eyes slam closed and his breathing huffs as if he's taken a physical blow, and I watch him try to pull himself together. "They died too easily."

He says it like it's a fact. I don't know how to respond.

16

He opens his eyes again, staring intensely at me, and I force myself to look back. "I swear to you, Marielle. You're free now forever. Neither they nor anyone else will ever hurt you again."

I wrap my arms around my belly, squeezing slightly. His eyes dart to track the movement, but then they return to my face.

It's been two hundred years. Two hundred years of this torture, of being cut up day after day, of being used.

I wonder if anyone thought I'd be this profitable when they first bought me.

I can hear footsteps, but then Callum snarls and they stop. I flinch away, and he turns his full attention back to me. "Sorry, Marielle, sorry, you're safe—"

The voice of the other man from the room, the brother, speaks. "I've sent for the cars," he calls from halfway across the lawn. "I'm going to light it up, and then we'll go."

Callum nods, not taking his eyes off me, but still speaking to his brother. "We can't make it home tonight," he says, loud enough for him to hear. "We need a hotel. New clothes. Everything Marielle might need. Maybe you can—"

"Honor already took a truck to go get it sorted," the brother interrupts, and then I hear his footsteps retreating towards the manor that I still don't want to look at.

After a moment, there's a brightness behind me, too bright to look at even if I wanted to.

Callum seems to know I don't want to see it, scooting closer on his knees so he takes up my entire field of vision. I force myself to hold my ground.

"What'll happen to me now?" I ask. Asking questions can be dangerous and rarely gets me the answers I'd like, but at the very least I can get some information, even if it's not answers to my questions, like how he'll respond, or what he'll do to me for asking.

"Now? Now we go home," he says, running a hand through his hair, pushing the waves every which way. His claws have shortened slightly, I notice absently, although I have no doubt they can do a lot of damage.

That's okay. I can take damage. I have been taking damage.

For the first time in hundreds of years, I can see. And there's no chain on my ankle, just a useless cuff that can't hold me. And I'm outside. I'm not in any pain, and even if that changes, even if that changes this very minute and I never have a pain-free moment again, I'll take what I can get.

"What's home?" I dare to ask.

"Home is our pack. My sister's pack, technically, but it's our pack. My sister is our queen."

I hitch a breath, eyes widening as I stare at him. That must make him a prince. Royalty.

What the hell could he want with me?

"And I'm coming with you?" I venture.

His eyes snap to mine with an intensity I can't name, piercing and making something inside me shiver. "Marielle. It's your home now too."

Home. He wouldn't call it my home if he meant it to be a new prison, would he?

He stares intensely for a moment, and I can't look away, but at last he shakes his head just slightly, seeming to dislodge his thoughts. "Honor is one of our soldiers. She's gone ahead to secure everything you might need for right now. And our ride will be here soon too."

"Horses?"

He winces. "Not exactly. You heard of a car?"

I've heard the term, but I couldn't picture one. I shrug.

"Right. Well. We'll show you. It'll be fine. For tonight, we'll go to a hotel, get you looked after. Tomorrow we'll go home."

I nod, not trusting myself to speak, not trusting myself to ask any questions. What do I know about any of this? I don't even know what a car is.

There's movement, and I focus on it, but he just picks up the jacket he'd discarded on the ground earlier, holding it open towards me. "You should put this on," he says quietly. "It's cold out here."

"Thank you." I let him guide me into the jacket. It's warm, made of leather, lined with something so soft it might as well be a cloud. I haven't felt something this nice in years.

He tugs on one side, straightening the jacket, before letting his hand run to my collarbones, then up to the side of my face, his eyes never leaving mine. "Anything you need, Marielle." His hand pushes my hair behind my ear, the gesture achingly gentle. Then his fingers freeze. "What's this?"

His fingertip rests gently on the pointed tip of my ear, unmoving, like his whole body froze.

Does he hate it? Do I care if he does?

His finger strokes carefully across the point. "Marielle?"

I move my head away from his touch, watching under my lashes to see how he reacts. He doesn't move. "I never knew my mother," I explain softly. "But I know she's one of the divine."

The divine, the children descended directly from gods. Near godly themselves, with talents far beyond what most of us could ever do. Humans have mistaken them for angels before, because they strike awe and fear into all who see them, supposedly.

I wouldn't know; I've never met one. I've never even met another halfling, the discarded remnants of the divine's trysts.

He doesn't move, doesn't so much as twitch, and I'm left wondering how he's taking that revelation.

Maybe he doesn't care. There's no reason he should care about me, after all.

"A halfling, then," he says after a long moment.

"Yes."

"Half what?"

"My father was a druid," I tell him.

"Explains the tree, then."

"I'm much more druid than divine," I hasten to say, not knowing why I feel this sudden need to explain. "Obviously. My mother left me with him. Wasn't special enough to keep, as you can see by me being trapped there."

I feel on uneven footing here, like the ground might fall out from beneath me, like I have no idea what to say. Maybe being druidic is less threatening and therefore more acceptable for him to keep. After all, if he wants to keep me for being half divine, then I'm sure I don't want to be kept. I wrap my arm around my stomach, thinking of the most recent incision there.

"I know a lot about plants," I say hesitantly. Maybe I have a value that doesn't lie in my body. "And I can draw energy from them like you saw. Use it for spellwork, especially healing." And poisons, but I don't mention it. "So, I can do that."

He just looks at me, and I get a sinking suspicion he doesn't understand what I'm trying to say. Is it because he already made up his mind about what I'll be useful for, and there's no use considering anything else? Or maybe they already have someone who does healing, and I'd be redundant.

"That's great," he says softly. "You'll have to show me. I don't really know anything about druids. But I'm excited to learn."

So I'm going with him after all, I think. And if he's serious—and everything about him seems sincere—then I will at least have enough freedom to use my gifts. That's something. I'll take that.

I don't have anywhere else to go, of course. I certainly can't go back to my father. And I have nowhere else. No friends, no family, no money to start over with.

And he looks at me with a softness in his eyes, even when he's tense, even when he's covered in blood. No one has ever looked at me with softness before.

It's the kind of thought my father would have hated. Life doesn't work like that. People aren't kind for free.

A movement draws my attention, and I see his hand, slowly held out towards me, palm up. I stare at it for a moment, probably too long, but I don't know what he wants.

He clears his throat. "Can I see your hand?"

I hasten to give it to him, not sure what he wants. Maybe there's something special about my hands. The claws are presumably from my mother's blood.

He gently runs a finger along my palm, then turns my hand so he can lace our fingers together, then runs his thumb soothingly along my knuckles. "Thank you."

I stare at our interlaced hands, not knowing what to say. Maybe I don't need to say anything.

A new light approaches us, different from the still-burning fire. Callum looks up sharply, and only then do I hear footsteps approaching again. The brother, I think.

"You two go ahead. Honor will meet you there. Jake will drive. The rest of us will catch up when this place is ash," he calls, not drawing any nearer.

Callum nods. "Can you walk, Marielle?" he asks me, standing and holding out his hand.

I nod, and he helps me to my feet, stopping only long enough to use his free hand to tug his jacket more fully around me. Given the state of my chemise, I'm grateful for any coverage it provides.

Callum hasn't made a single inappropriate comment, nor a single inappropriate touch. Even when he found me where he did. Even when he has to be aware of how they all used me.

He leads me to what must be the car, a hulking black box on wheels with the bright light emitting from the front. He goes and opens a door in the back, gesturing me in, and then slides in after me.

"Jake," he says, turning only half his attention to the front, "Drive fast, alright?"

I don't look up to see who he's talking to. I just look at our hands, once again intertwined, and feel the rumble of the car under me as we leave this prison, hopefully forever.

.

CHAPTER SIX

MARIELLE

The car moves fast, scenery speeding by the windows. Soon enough, the fire is too far behind us for me to still see.

That eases something in me, but I can't relax completely. As large as the car is, Callum still looks hulking in the backseat, like he's simply too large for the space. And as I keep my attention on him, I can't forget about the second wolf in the front seat.

Callum looks me over unhappily, and I shrink from his sight. But all he says is, "You must be cold."

I swallow. "I'm alright." Cold? I can't remember the last time I wasn't.

He must know what I haven't said. Or maybe I was just meant to agree with him, because his frown deepens, but he just shakes his head. "We're not going too far to the hotel, and Honor'll have some better clothes for you."

"Thank you," I manage to say.

He looks at me intensely for a minute, then nods. "Anything else you need, let me know, alright? Or any of us. I'll take care of it."

What could I need? I don't even know what I need. Clothes would be nice. I can't remember the last time I had a new dress. A place to sleep besides the ground would be wonderful.

"Here," the man from the front says. Jake, they called him. He tosses something back, and Callum takes it. It's silver and makes a crinkling sound as he unfolds it until he has a large silver square.

"Shock blanket," he explains when he sees me looking. "Modern invention. It keeps in heat but can be folded small enough to travel easily. They're meant when a patient needs to keep their heat up. We use them when a wolf gets hit hard, to stabilize them when they heal."

I look at it with slightly more interest now. Healing. I know a little about that. Not that I'd been a healer, but I knew a fair amount of medicines and poisons. It had been my father's primary business, after all.

I'd spent hours feeling for the strongest plants, drawing forth the best ingredients, mixing them correctly to save or kill, whatever was called for. And I liked it well enough, especially the healing side.

I don't really understand why Jake gave it to him, though. If it's for wolves injured in battle, then neither of the wolves in this car qualifies. But then he spreads it over my lap.

"I'm not injured." Not anymore, anyway.

"But you are cold, and this'll hold the heat in until we can do better," he says, going to tuck the blanket in around my leg. He frowns when he gets to the metal cuff still on my ankle. "Didn't want to scare you earlier, but think I can try to take this off?"

"It's enchanted."

He looks up, raising an eyebrow. "You said the chain was enchanted too."

Arrogant wolf. But he's not wrong. And while I barely notice the cuff, as used to it as I am...

I nod. If it's gone, if I get new clothes, if I go somewhere else, could I really start fresh? Leave all that in the past, in the ashes that manor is no doubt becoming right now?

"Hold still," he warns me, then gently cups my leg, swinging it so it's in his lap. I tense, thinking of all the ways he could hurt me like this. Even with his grip as gentle as if he was holding a butterfly's wings, he still moved me so easily.

He uses one hand to grip my ankle, and the other to grip the cuff, and then moves with speed I wouldn't expect from his large frame. I bite my lip against the yelp as the metal pulls against my skin, but when I look down, the cuff is gone.

I can't stop staring. For the first time in centuries...

Callum rubs gently over the skin. "Glad that's taken care of," he says, and then carefully tucks my leg back under the silver blanket.

All I can do is stare at him as he sits back in his seat. Then, he opens the window by simply pressing a button, and tosses the broken cuff out the window before closing it again.

I gape at him, unable to help it.

What in the hell does this all mean? What kind of person does this for someone like me?

"How long until we get there, Jake?" Callum asks, interrupting my thoughts.

"'Bout twenty minutes."

Callum nods, then turns his attention back to me. "I didn't hurt you, did I?"

All I can do is shake my head and keep watching him, trying to figure out what any of this means.

***

At the hotel, Jake parks the car in a sea of other cars, and then Callum carries me around to the side of a building. "Honor already got the room," he explains, even if I didn't ask. "And she'll be waiting with the key, so you don't have to go through the lobby."

I look down at myself, still wrapped in that blanket and Callum's coat, feet bare, and concede that it's probably best I don't walk through a room full of humans.

The room is at the end of an opulent hallway on the third level, and a tall, dark-haired woman waits there for us. She frowns when she sees us, but nods at Callum. "I should have everything to get through the night. I'll get more when you've settled in," she says.

She does something behind her back and the door swings open to reveal a room just as lavish as the hallway. Once she steps inside and Callum follows suit, she turns to me. "Marielle?"

"Hello." She smiles when I say it.

"Want to get cleaned up?"

What does cleaned up mean? If I'm lucky, it'll mean a bath. I nod.

And then nothing happens for a long moment, until Honor chuckles. "Gonna have to let her go, there, boss-man," she says, her voice teasing.

Callum grips me tighter for a minute and I'm worried he'll refuse, but then he sets me on my feet, the silver blanket falling away.

Honor takes me in with an unsubtle sweep of her eyes. "Think I got the right sizes. But if anything doesn't fit, just let us know. We'll replace it. Now, let's see about getting cleaned up."

I nod and move to follow her. Callum stays put, and even with Honor's warm smile guiding me forward, I somehow feel colder.

CHAPTER SEVEN

CALLUM

Honor didn't skimp on anything Marielle might need.

She told us it was enough for tonight, but I think Marielle is overwhelmed with what Honor thinks is necessary to just start out. There's a variety of clothing, toiletries, new shoes, and even some books. I make a mental note to make sure Honor gets reimbursed.

Not that this shopping spree will break the bank of a well-regarded pack enforcer like Honor, who's had as long as I have to build up both reputation and wealth, but it's the principle of the thing. I will be the one to provide for my mate.

I'd like to be providing for her right now, in the bath. I'd like to be the one who cleans her, pampers her, who winces over every little cut that might still be on her skin, who uncovers every inch of her.

Instead, I'm seated on the other side of the bathroom door, listening.

Honor talked her through the modern fixtures in the bathroom, the skin care and haircare products, and some of the clothes, and then left her to it. Honor had closed the door, looked long and hard at me, rolled her eyes, and gone to leave, saying only she'd send room service with food.

Eye roll or no eye roll, Honor knows what the mating bond can do to a wolf. Her mate waits for her at home, and I sincerely doubt either of them were any better than I am right now when it first happened a century ago.

So I wait, listening to the sound of bottles being uncapped and the light splashing of water. About five minutes ago, I heard the drain being unplugged, and soon after the rustling of a towel.

I can hear fabric moving again. Clothes this time, I think.

I can smell her through the door. I could probably smell her across the city, to be honest. She smells different now. Better. Cleaner, yes, like there's been something marring her scent, and now it's just her left behind.

I want to bury my face in her neck, her hair, her thighs, the places her scent will be strongest. I want to breathe nothing else forever.

I pinch my thigh, reminding myself not to say shit like that to her face. Not yet.

Although we believe everyone has a fated mate, not everyone can feel it instinctively. The wolves do, and the demons. Vampires too, I think. Everyone else has to work for it.

The moment I smelled her, I knew. But she'll have to be wooed first.

That's fine. I am more than up for wooing my mate.

It's only complicated by the other half of her identity. Divine. I've met very few divine in my life, and I'm a thousand years old. I've met a few of their halflings, like Marielle, but even those are rare.

I don't know shit about the divine. I know they think they're above the rest of us. I know they descend directly from gods and are powerful for it. I know they're a lethal enemy to have. But I don't know how they mate, or if they take eternal mates.

I've never heard of a divine parent sticking with their halfling's other parent, so I'm guessing not.

I hear footsteps and scramble away from the door, moving over to the couch to make it look like I've been casually hanging out over here. The door opens, and I look up.

And barely stop my mouth from dropping.

For someone who had never met Marielle before, Honor shopped well. The t-shirt fits her like a second skin, hugging plump breasts and a softly rounded belly. And the leggings look painted on, drawing my attention straight to her hips.

If she turns around, I'd be willing to bet her ass just might kill me.

Marielle shifts from foot to foot, and I trail my eyes over her whole body, from her small little feet now encased in fuzzy socks, to her legs, her hips, her stomach, her breasts, her face. She's frowning, and everything in me aches to soothe it. My mate shouldn't have cause to frown.

"Is this what people dress like now?"

I have to clear my throat to be able to speak clearly. "It's one way people dress," I say. "But there's options. And you can dress however you like." I try to think about what women wore two hundred years ago. Were corsets in style then? It's hard to remember, because Celia and Bethany aren't big followers of human fashion, and most women I see are on the battlefield and training ground. But it doesn't matter. Whatever was in style then, she can have it. I'll find someone who will make that for her, and I'm sure I'll find it just as damn alluring as I do these leggings.

She shrugs. "It's comfortable. And more than I had. I'm grateful for that." She looks around the suite. "Where's Honor?"

"She went to her own room. Do you need her?"

She shakes her head, slowly. "Oh, no. I'm glad she went to rest. I just wanted to thank her."

"I'll pass it along."

She fidgets again. The little movement of her hips as she does so should be cute, but I ache to see it, the unsureness in her face. "I don't mean to keep you. If you'd also like to go rest, please don't feel like you need to help me."

Like my entire existence isn't dedicated to helping her in whatever way she'd like me to. I don't say it. It's too early.

I clear my throat and point behind me. "That's my room," I tell her, then pointing across the living room of the suite, "and that's yours. I'll leave you alone if you'd like, but a meal should be here shortly."

She frowns. "I don't eat."

Well. That's unexpected. And a little unwanted, truth be told. Providing food for a mate is a time-honored wolf tradition, after all.

"At all?"

She shrugs, not looking at me. "Not since I stopped aging. They stopped feeding me then."

My heart nearly stops, and the food is forgotten. "They... you were with them before you stopped aging?" When she was a child? When she was vulnerable and not yet fully immortal?

Where was I? I demand furiously of myself. I know I wouldn't have recognized her as my mate then, that I couldn't have recognized a child, but logic doesn't apply here. Logic means nothing in the face of realizing what's been done to her.

"I was sixteen. And it was easier then. They couldn't hurt me as badly. It wouldn't re-grow. And they wanted to make sure I would be able to supply them for a long, long time to come," she murmurs.

Sixteen. A child. Vulnerable. Mortal.

She spent anywhere from four to fourteen years mortal in their custody. I look her over, eyeing the body immortality froze for her, and guess she spent eight or nine years mortal.

The silence between us hangs heavy and hot, and she starts to fidget again. I force myself to speak, to turn the attention away from the subject making her uncomfortable. "You can't eat food, or just don't need to?"

She shrugs. "I haven't eaten since I became immortal, so... I don't know."

"Would you like to try?"

She seems to consider it, head tilted. "I wouldn't want to be an inconvenience."

She's too precious. And also not demanding enough. It's going to take time to get her to understand that everything I have, everything I could provide, is hers. And I'm a millennium old. I have a lot to provide.

"They'll deliver it to our door," I say, which takes some of the pride out of providing for my mate, but at least it might convince her it's not some great inconvenience. "And it should be here any minute. If I know Honor, and I do, she ordered plenty for even a wolf like me to eat well, and then some. There'll be food for you."

She smiles at me. It's small, and it fades quickly, but it's the first smile I've seen and it almost brings me to my knees. I'll do anything to see another one. "Alright," she says, then pauses for a moment. "Thank you."

I should tell her not to thank me, that it's all already hers, but I know she isn't prepared to hear it. "You're welcome, Marielle." I gesture to the couch, and she thankfully sits.

I leave plenty of space between us, even as it hurts to do so. I don't want to crowd her or scare her away. But I can't help dreaming of the future. Where she might cuddle into my side, using my bulk to keep herself warm. Or where she might throw her legs over my lap, letting me massage out the aches from the day. Or where she might fall asleep there, leaning against me, and let me carry her to bed.

I pinch my thigh hard, digging my claws in, when I think about her trailing a hand up my thigh. Teasing. Stroking. Tempting. I force myself to stop before I imagine sliding to my knees on the floor, throwing her legs over my shoulders, and ripping those leggings from her body.

I pinch hard enough to draw blood. It won't show through the dark jeans, and she thankfully is too busy looking around the room to notice.

Her shirt has ridden up, exposing a few inches of that beautiful belly. I want to rest my head there, want to press a thousand kisses to the skin, want to hold her waist and—

Woo her, I remind myself. Not whatever this is. This will just scare her away.

I should call my brother. Bryce might know a thing or two about being patient, about wooing a fated mate who doesn't feel the pull the same way we do. Maybe he has some advice.

If he can be pulled away from his honeymoon long enough to give it.

Like I summoned it, my phone dings. I look down, but it's Heath.

Whenever you get a moment, we need to know what she knows about them.

Fuck.

I look up at her. She looks soft like this, sitting on the overstuffed couch, wearing leggings and fuzzy socks. She looks almost like she's forgotten the horrors of the last few centuries, although I'd be an idiot to think that's actually true.

Even so, she looks like the new world, her future, is engaging enough to distract her. But I have to be the asshole that reminds her of the past.

Heath could do it. I could call Heath back in here, or Honor even, and I could sit there and be supportive and not have to ask her the hard questions.

But I don't want them near my mate, not tonight. I don't want her to be forced to tell anyone but me what she went through; I don't want anyone who will not be infinitely understanding asking her questions. I don't think I could let them hurt her, even like this.

I have to be the one to question her.

CHAPTER EIGHT

MARIELLE

I watch him watch the little box in his hand. Honor had one too, I think.

He catches me looking and smiles softly at me. That one gesture makes his face so gentle, in a way I can't quite imagine.

None of the rest of him is gentle. He still hasn't changed his clothes, so there's blood on him. He's one of the tallest people I've ever seen, close to six and a half feet tall. He dwarfs me. I could stand behind him and be completely invisible to everyone else. His arms look like they can and do regularly break other people, and probably people as big as he is.

But his smile and his eyes are gentle, and I'm finding myself less and less scared of him with every minute that passes.

"What is that?" I dare to ask, nodding at the device in his hand.

"It's a phone. A communication device?" he says, seeing my confusion. "We can send messages, in writing or with voice. My brother sent me a text message."

Text messages. Alright then.

Honor talked me through a lot of the features of the hotel room and the things she bought me. I've seen cars, and now phones. I'll piece this new modern world together if it's the last thing I do.

He continues. "Heath—my brother—was reminding me that I... we... need to ask you some questions. About the group who held you hostage. I know it's not going to be a conversation you want to have, but..."

But they need to know. I nod and try not to let the fear show on my face.

It's an unpleasant story, but I owe it to them. And if this is all they ask of me, if this is the only pain they demand of me... well, I should consider myself lucky.

He tilts his head and just looks at me for a long moment, and I wish he'd just ask. Get it over with.

How many times will I need to re-tell it, though? Once for Callum, once for Heath. Maybe again for his sister, the queen, if she even has time for nobodies like me.

What do they need to know? Maybe they're just looking for how to duplicate the spells. Maybe they're wondering what pieces of me they need to cut off.

I instinctively put a hand over my stomach, as if I can protect myself, and Callum clearly watches the movement. He frowns, and I shrink back.

"You must have questions too," he decides. "If you answer mine, I'll answer yours."

It's a worthwhile deal, and one he didn't need to make. I would have answered his questions anyway. I have to; I've already more than taken advantage of his goodwill and hospitality.

"You ask first," I say softly, still holding my stomach.

His frown only deepens. "Are you hurt?"

"No."

"You're holding your stomach."

I swallow. "Just remembering."

"They cut from you there?"

"They cut from me everywhere. I think I've re-grown everything a dozen times over at least. Some parts of me were more needed than others. Sometimes they took my eyes whole, so they could use them. Sometimes my liver or my ribs. Fingers were common. My spleen, sometimes."

I watch his hand ball into a fist. It should frighten me, but something tells me it's not intended for me.

Besides, I've long since learned that the worst pain doesn't come from a balled fist, and that a person doesn't need to be big to cause me hurt.

"What did they use it for?"

"Spells. Not spells like I do, a different type of magic, so I don't really understand, but—spells."

It should be my turn to ask a question, but I don't dare interrupt.

"What kind of spells? Do you remember any of them?" He looks at me intently, and even leans forward a bit, so I guess this is the important question.

But I can't help him. I wish I could; I wish I knew whatever he wanted to know. It would be a good thing to have something to trade, something worth knowing. But I just don't.

"They never told me." They never told me anything, truth be told. They cut from me or they used me or they ignored me. That was it.

He sighs and settles back. "That's okay, Marielle. It was a long-shot."

"You know, though," I hazard a guess. "What were they doing?" What were they using my body for?

He closes his eyes for a long second, then nods. "We were sent in because we'd started to hear about enslavement spells."

It's like the sofa falls away from beneath me, like the ground collapses. I knew they were bad people. They hurt me, cut me, tortured me, used me. But enslavement spells...

I know they existed. I know it all too well, can still remember the light leaving Theo's eyes.

My grip on my stomach tightens. My body was used to do that to people.

He seems to read it on my face. "Yeah. Would have been convenient if you knew how they worked. So we could start figuring out how to stop them."

"Sorry."

"Don't be sorry, Marielle. You don't know. No one can blame you for that."

Perhaps they can't blame me, but what value do I hold if I don't know the one thing they want to know?

"What questions do you have for me?" he asks, interrupting my worry.

I stop and consider. I know he's a wolf, and he must be some sort of warrior. I know he's incredibly strong, that he has a brother and a sister at least, that he's royalty. I know he's said I'll be coming home with them.

But that was before I was useless.

"Am I really coming home with you?"

"Yes." His answer is almost immediate.

"Why? I can't do anything for you." I hold my stomach again, as if my arm could stop him. Unless they want me for whenever they do figure out how to do the spell.

No. The spell disgusts him, I can tell. He wouldn't want to perform it himself, if he even could.

Callum tilts his head, looking me over. "It's not about doing anything. It'll never be about doing anything," he says fiercely. "There's no expectations."

"Then what is it about?" His own ferocity is making me bold. Too bold, maybe. But there's nothing to lose right now.

It's almost like he stutters to a stop, mouth open and no words emerging. He stops, swallows, and tries again. "You deserve to go somewhere safe, Marielle."

He's keeping something from me. I can see it in his eyes, in his hesitation. But I don't push yet. "And you're safe?"

He nods quickly, then slides to the floor, moving on his knees until he's in front of me. He reaches out for a moment, then lets his hands drop. "I swear, Marielle. You will always be safe with me. Always." He doesn't get off his knees, and I look down at him, unsure what to do with this. He's staring back at me, his brown eyes so big and soft.

"You won't hurt me?"

"Never. And no one else will, either." He manages a small smile. "You might've noticed I'm a big fucker, Marielle. I swear no one will get through me. No one will ever cut you again."

He can't promise that. He can't always be there. He's royalty, he's a warrior. He probably has a mate, or will someday. But that's okay. I don't need him to defend me always. Once upon a time, I was able to do that for myself.

There's one more thing I want to ask. If he'll touch me like they did, use me like they did. But I don't.

He winces. "Sorry about the language."

He's managed to startle a laugh out of me. "I've heard worse."

"From them?"

"Sometimes. But my brother also swore frequently." He had enough reason to, after all.

"You have a brother?"

He's still on his knees, and I have a feeling it will be awhile before he notices any physical discomfort, but I still don't like it. "I did," I say. "He's probably dead now. Would you come sit up here?"

He moves immediately, sliding to the seat next to me. He leaves space, but with the size of him, it still feels like he's surrounding me.

I don't dislike it, and I wonder what that says.

"Why would your brother be dead?"

"He was human," I tell him, and I suppress a laugh as he tries to work that one out. "He wasn't my brother by blood in any way. I've seen slave spells before. Because Theo, he was my father's slave." I wince, trying to remember Theo. It's been so, so long since I've seen his face. "I helped him run away when I was fifteen. He had a suitor waiting. And I never saw him again."

"Must've been hard."

"It wasn't long until... well, until I was taken."

The silence between us is uncomfortable, and I don't want to sit in uncomfortable silence. Besides, he said I could ask questions. "Your siblings. Tell me about them."

His soft smile returns, and everything in me relaxes at the sight. "Celia is our queen. She's the oldest, even if it's only by a few minutes. Then Bryce, then Heath. They're triplets. You met Heath. And I have three siblings-by-fate: Bethany is mated to Celia, Mae and Bryce mated a few years ago, and Heath is mated to Chase."

He doesn't introduce a mate of his own, and while I've never met wolves before tonight, everything I've heard told me he would have mentioned his own mate first, above even his queen. "You're the youngest sibling?"

He grins, wide and bright, and I want to see it more. His eyes crinkle up in the corners, and I want to touch the lines there. "I'm the baby. By almost fifty years.

So you can imagine what that was like." I can't, really. Theo was my only sibling, and he was both not my actual brother and my father's servant. He was kind to me, taught me things I understand an older sibling should, but he left without looking back and I don't blame him.

But that's okay. I can see the joy and the love in Callum's eyes.

"Mae is incredibly young," he continues. "She's barely sixty. So I'm not the youngest anymore, by almost a thousand years. You'll like her, I think. She's a witch, so she might get your magical stuff."

Witches and druids are different types of casters. Witches are deliberate, driving their spells through their own power and external components. They need to assemble spells. Druids just channel nature energy. But it would be nice to meet another caster who isn't trying to carve out my liver.

"Chase is a caster too, but demon magic is very different."

"One of your brothers-by-fate is a demon?"

"Yeah. He's a good man. He and Heath make a good pair."

Their home must be something else. I want to ask him again why he'd welcome me into this family he so clearly loves. What worth I have, what I'd be able to contribute. But he already answered, and I hesitate to ask again.

There's a knock on the door, and I freeze.

Callum sniffs once, then stands, unfolding himself from the couch gracefully. "Food's here," he says, crossing the room towards the door.

I haven't eaten anything since the day I froze into immortality, and didn't eat very much before that. But Callum is so insistent that I eat, and I hesitantly stand to follow him.

CHAPTER NINE

CALLUM

I use my body to block the door, both stopping the man pushing the cart of food from seeing Marielle and stopping him from entering. The way things are going, I'm liable to hurt anyone unknown who enters my mate's space right now.

This hotel room isn't a den, but my wolf brain is treating it like it is, and I can't help it.

It's not just that she's a new mate, although that's part of it. It's that she won't stop holding her stomach, protecting her soft belly, like she expects someone to come at her with a knife any second.

Not to mention, every word she said to me has hinted why her scent changed after her bath. I just haven't worked up the courage to ask her yet.

Maybe I should let Celia ask her. Let another woman do it. Maybe it'll make her feel safer.

Plus, if I hear about someone raping my mate, I'm going to tear someone's head off.

Not hers. I won't lay a finger on her, will die before I do, and before I let anyone else do it, either. But I know I'm big, and I know I'm scary to look at. I don't want to give her any reason to be scared.

I tip the man and wheel the cart in myself, making sure to keep my body between Marielle and the door. The man is a human, no doubt about it, but I can't be too careful.

Celia nearly ripped my head off for accidentally hurting Bethany during sword practice a thousand or so years ago. I thought she was over-exaggerating then.

I probably owe all three of my siblings apologies, given that I now finally understand what it is to have a mate. To have someone to kill and die and live for, to have someone who takes up your whole heart.

I present her with the cart of food, smiling. "Take whatever you want."

She stares at it blankly. "What is all of it?"

Right. I roll it over to the table in the suite and start setting dishes on the tables, showing off what we have, naming food as I go.

It looks like Honor ordered the entire menu. Probably the right call, considering that a wolf can eat a shocking amount after they've expended a lot of energy. And the battle wasn't necessarily a taxing one, but the gesture is nice.

Wolves aren't big on propriety. I hand her a knife and fork, and say, "Dig in. Have a little bit of everything if you want. As much as you want. And if you need to know what it is, I'll tell you."

I don't wait around to watch, thinking my staring might make her uncomfortable, and grab my own utensils before starting on a steak and fries meal, shoving an uncomfortable amount of steak in my mouth.

Table manners, Callum. She's probably grossed out.

But when I look over, she's not even watching me. She's chewing thoughtfully. A French fry, I think, judging by the plate she's pulled closer. "Good?" I ask when I've managed to swallow my mouthful.

"Good," she says, after she's chewed and swallowed much more elegantly than I did.

Everything about her seems small and elegant, and I wonder how fate paired me with her. I'm not a brute, necessarily, but I've spent my whole life at war. I've fought for my pack and all wolves for centuries. I've led special operations like tonight for just as long. I've trained with swords and knives and axes and claws and teeth. She seems small, almost fragile, next to me.

Maybe I can train her. Maybe that's what fate knows I can do for her. I can train her so she never has to feel like she has been feeling again.

And if she doesn't want that, well, I'll always be there to protect her. She never has to worry about someone hurting her again.

Because I'll break them into pieces. I'll rip their throats out and present them as gifts.

She bites into another French fry, and I can't stop myself from watching. Not even the call of more steak can take my attention from her.

"So, you can eat then," I venture, forcing myself to spear more food as she finishes.

"It seems so."

"Good. I'm glad. Food is enjoyable, and you deserve to enjoy it."

She sets aside the fork she's been using to eat French fries. Wait until I introduce her to ketchup.

"I don't understand why you're so concerned about me," she admits. "I'm nothing to you."

You're everything, I barely resist saying. Everything. "You've been through something awful," I say simply.

"You've never met anyone who's been through something awful before? I thought as a warrior you'd meet a lot of us. Or do you take us all home?"

I exhale deeply. Shit, she's got me there. She's astute. "Yeah, I..." I don't have a good answer for her. Not without telling her the truth, at least.

Would it be so bad? Would it scare her? Maybe it would reassure her. Assure her of her place here, that nothing will make me let her go, that nothing will ever stop me from protecting her.

Or it would chase her away. And I can't risk that. Not until I know her better.

"I like to help people," I manage to say. Not a lie, necessarily, which is good, because I don't want to lie to my mate. "And I don't like seeing people go through such awful things."

Her eyes stare right through me, and I make myself hold her gaze.

She looks away first. "Thank you."

I swallow. "You're very welcome, Marielle. And don't worry—it'll all get better from here."

Her nose scrunches slightly, like she's not sure what I mean.

That's okay. I'll show her.

***

I convince her to go to bed when we finish the food. I ate the majority, but she ate some, picking her way through a salad and a curry dish and her fair share of the french fries. Good. Even if she technically doesn't require it, I rather know she has a full belly and feels good.

Those sick fucks must have loved that she didn't need to eat. One more way to deprive her.

They probably took it for granted, though. After all, she's a divine halfling. That has to be why they wanted her. Something special in her, in her blood.

And every other bit of her body they could cut out, I think sourly.

Speaking of divine halfling, I'm in sudden need of a crash course of everything about them.

I know their other parent's species can have a big impact, and that every halfling is a little different. But I need to learn whatever I can. I suddenly find myself responsible for a halfling, and her health, safety, and happiness are now my top priority.

I pull out my phone and text Heath.

Can you ask Chase to ask Ryder to ask Hannah some questions?

It takes him less than a minute to respond. One crash course about halflings coming up. But you know Demonheim means communication will be slow.

I do know that. But I love him for being willing to play the trans-dimensional game of phone tag for me anyway.

That's the thing about mates. We all understand. We all long for the day we find ours and celebrate everyone else who does. And we'll move heaven and earth to support each other through this.

I tuck my phone away, looking around the room. I don't know who booked it, Heath or Honor or someone else, but I'm more than grateful. It's a nice suite, with all the luxuries I'd want my mate to know she deserves and that she can expect now.

There are two bedrooms, but I have no intention of sleeping in mine. If I even do fall asleep, this couch will be fine. I need to be closer to her.

It's normal for newly mated wolves to be on high alert, I remind myself. Wanting to be between her and anyone who can come through the door is normal.

What's not normal is how badly my mate has been hurt. And even if we did kill every fucker in that place—I doubt Heath left until he was sure—I'm still tense.

Besides. I want to be closer in case she needs anything.

Like that thought summoned it, I hear a whimper and shoot to my feet, pushing open the door she left ajar and entering her room.

I swallow. Nightmare.

The blankets are tangled around her legs, and her hands are thrown wide, scrambling, fighting something. Her face scrunches up with remembered pain.

I force myself to move forward slowly, quietly. I want to wake her from her nightmare, but I don't delude myself into thinking her waking with me looming over her, being loud and aggressive and so wolfish, will in any way soothe her.

She's already half convinced I'll hurt her. I'd prefer not to confirm her fears accidentally.

I kneel next to her bed, reaching for one of the fighting hands and taking it gently in mine, running fingers along the back of it, tracing the delicate skin. After a moment, the muscles in her hand relax, and then a minute later, the rest of her body relaxes too.

When was the last time anyone touched my mate with kindness?

I swallow. I will touch her with kindness. I will show her a family, a community, a life, of kindness. And she will never have to know an unkind touch again.

"Be at ease, Marielle," I murmur, so quietly the words are more a rumble in my chest than an actual sound. "Nothing will hurt you here. I'll be between you and danger."

I don't sleep that night. I sit on her floor, holding that delicate hand as gently as I possibly can, sitting between her and anything in the outside world. She has no more nightmares. And when dawn comes, I creep out quietly, before she wakes.

Chapter Ten

Marielle

"Tell me about your home?" I ask quietly the next morning.

We're in the car again. Callum stops eating what he called a protein bar immediately. He'd insisted we have breakfast at the hotel—more food I didn't need, an absolutely decadent luxury—but it's been a few hours. I imagine someone as big as him needs a lot of food to keep himself going.

He sets the bar down and turns to me fully, and I squirm under the full weight of his attention.

Being noticed, having someone pay attention, has never been a good thing. Being noticed meant I was going to be hurt. It at least meant my father would find some fault to complain about. I'd always considered it better to slip under anyone's notice. It was safer, at least.

Callum looks at me and seems to see more than anyone else has. And I feel safe regardless.

It's his eyes, and some part of me wants to touch the lines around them, the softness I see there.

No one's ever looked at me like that.

Maybe Theo. He was as soft with me as he could be, I think. But it never felt like this.

"What do you want to know?" he asks.

I shrug. "Just... tell me about it. I haven't..." Haven't ever had a home, I don't say.

"We're pretty far north," he tells me. "So it's going to be on the cooler side. But it gives us a lot of land, relatively isolated from humans. Allows us space to run and just not have to fear and keep everything so secret."

"That must be nice."

"It's convenient. And we've needed the space too. There's wolves all over the world these days, but this is our historic home, and there're plenty of us still there."

I think about that, how large the community might be.

Will I be able to blend in and disappear in a large community? Or will I stick out?

"Where will I be staying?"

"With me," he says immediately, as if he's already thought about it. "About the time Heath came home with Chase, we all decided the one big house model wasn't going to work anymore. It was bad enough hearing Celia and Bethany, but two happy couples was just too much. So we changed things up. It was time to modernize anyways. And now we each have our own home. I have plenty of room. And the rest of the family is still right there, so you're not just stuck with me. I have a feeling you'll like them."

"You don't need to..." I trail off. He doesn't need to take care of me, and I don't want to be a burden. But where would I go instead? It's not like I have relations to take me in, and I certainly can't afford a home.

"It's a big house, Marielle," he says. "Trust me, you're not putting me out. I'd be honored to have you."

Honored. Like there's anything great about me being in his space. Like I'm worth it.

He turns half his attention to the front of the car, although I can still feel him watching me. "What about it, Jake? I miss anything about the town?"

Jake, who's been driving relatively silently this whole time, snorts. "So much," he says. "But see for yourself."

We crest a large hill, and I crane my neck to look into the valley below.

It's green and lush with fresh spring growth. My eyes go to the trees and flowers and grasses first, but then I see the houses. There's a crowded town center, and then houses become more and more sporadic as they move outwards, with plenty of land.

I can see people, far away and small, moving about their daily lives. Wolves, probably. I wonder if any of the people I see are Callum's family.

Thinking of him, I turn back to him, to see him watching me, grinning. "It's a nice place," he offers.

"It's beautiful." And I mean it. I don't know how long this will last, don't know what value I hold in being brought here, but I'm honored I've gotten to come.

We move down the hill, into the valley. Jake clears his throat. "Heath asked me to take you to Celia's house," he says. "You good with that?"

"Sure, whatever," Callum says absently, still watching me.

I'm going to have to meet the queen right away.

I look down at myself. I'm wearing yet another pair of the leggings Honor brought me, and a sweater that seems too big but makes me feel soft and protected. Not clothes to meet a queen.

I don't own clothes to meet a queen, I remind myself.

Maybe she'll be understanding. She has to know I was a prisoner not twenty-four hours ago, that I'm her youngest brother's charity project. Maybe she'll forgive me for the disrespect, and I'll still have time to win her over later.

"You'll like Celia," Callum says, as if he's unaware of my turmoil. But I look back up at him, and he's watching me closely, so maybe he's more aware than I thought. "She's a good leader to this pack. And I'm sure Bethany'll be there, too."

"Bethany is your sister-by-fate?"

"Yeah. She and Celia mated pretty young, all things considered, so she's as much family as any of them. I mean, all siblings-by-fate are. But I've known Bethany almost my whole life."

The car stops in front of a big house. I thought the queen would live close to the center of the town, but she lives closer to the road down the hill, which seems to be the only entrance to the small community.

45

Callum gets out of the car while I'm still looking, then comes to my door to open it, extending a hand to help me out. I take it, stepping down from the car, looking around.

He doesn't let go of my hand, but uses his free hand to gesture to the right. "Our house is about a hundred yards that way. When we built them, we decided we'd essentially build a perimeter defense. And give ourselves a little bit of space. I'll show you after, but we shouldn't keep Celia waiting."

He doesn't drop my hand, instead cradling it as he shows me to the house. He doesn't bother to knock as he lets himself in.

"Celia, we're here."

"Good, whole gang's here now," a woman says, walking out of a room down the hall.

I look her over. She's not any taller than I am, with dark hair done up in elaborate twists and buns. The clothes she's wearing reveal more skin than they hide. It presents as a dress, but a dress with a slit that shows off almost all of her thick thighs and plunges low over her ample cleavage.

If this is the queen, then I suppose I don't have to be worried about my own clothing choices.

Callum's hand briefly tightens on mine. "Mae. When did you get here?"

She shrugs. "Heath called your brother last night, and Chase came to get us. We're all here."

A man emerges behind Mae. He's as tall as Callum. Looks like him too, with dark wavy hair and brown eyes, although his hair is cut shorter. He looks down at Mae, sliding a hand around her waist. Even with Mae's thick stomach, that hand looks huge on her body. Callum's equally large hand suddenly feels warmer around mine.

"Bryce," Callum says. "You didn't have to come back."

Bryce looks up from Mae long enough to give his brother a rather intense stare. "Don't be stupid," he says, before turning to me. "You must be Marielle."

I nod, swallowing, trying to find my words. "I—yes. Pleasure to meet you."

When I was young, a curtsy might have been appropriate, but I'm hardly wearing a skirt.

"Pleasure's all ours," Mae pipes in, and she gives me a smile that changes her entire face, making it soft and welcoming. "I hear you're a druid, right? Caster's gotta stick together. Have you met Chase yet?"

Chase was the demon brother-by-fate, if I remember correctly. I shake my head no. "Well, let's change that," Mae says, and then she turns to look up at her mate, smiling at him tenderly. "Lead the way, big guy."

He leans down to kiss her softly before moving his hand to wrap his arm around her shoulders, pulling her into his side as they walk.

Callum catches my eye and then rolls his eyes. "Three and a half years and you'd think they met yesterday," he whispers.

"I can hear you," Bryce says, not turning his attention from his mate at all.

"Valid criticism though," Callum responds.

Mae snorts. "You'll understand soon, Callum."

I frown. Callum doesn't have a mate. Surely he would have mentioned them by now if he did.

Before I can decide if I should ask, Bryce and Mae reach a big wooden door, and Bryce pushes it open.

He's big enough to block most of the doorway, but when he moves out of the way, Mae still at his side, I get a view inside.

The office is spacious, with a large, currently unlit fireplace, multiple sofas and chairs, and an intimidating wooden desk by the window. Bryce and Mae move over to the sofas by the fireplace, joining everyone else waiting.

I recognize Heath, even if I never got a great look at him. He's as tall as his brothers, as broad as them, too. I know Callum is the younger brother, but the three boys could have been the triplets. Heath has a large scar cutting through his left eye, and I feel an instant empathy, remembering the agonizing feeling of losing my own eyes. His eye is still there, but it moves slower as he turns towards us.

Someone sits on Heath's right, his hand casually on Heath's knee, and I realize after a moment he has small horns barely poking out from his hair. Chase, then. He's not as big as the three brothers, but he'd still tower over me.

On the other couch are two women, and I can pick out the queen instantly. She looks a lot like her brothers, with dark hair and brown eyes. She might not be as tall as they are, but I bet she's six feet tall at least when she's standing.

I'm relieved that I'm apparently not underdressed to meet the queen. She's wearing denim pants like Callum is, and a button-down shirt that does very little to hide how muscular she is.

The last person must be Bethany, Celia's mate. She sits back comfortably on the couch, taking in the room. She's paler than snow, with hair so light it's almost white, and she smiles wide when she sees me looking.

The silence hangs in the room for a long moment, and then Celia stands, walking over to us. I was right about her size, and I have to look up to see her. "Welcome to our pack, Marielle," she says. Her voice is very serious, but her smile is bright and welcoming.

"Thank you," I manage to force out, hoping my voice stays even and I don't sound like a fool. "I'm so pleased to be here." An understatement.

"We're pleased to have you," she says, her voice still serious. Maybe she always is. I can't imagine being a queen is an easy task.

A throat clears from the couch and we all turn to see Bethany stand. She's not as tall as her mate, but she's close. Celia is built like her brothers, muscled and clearly ready to go to war any minute. Bethany is thinner, more willowy.

"We're thrilled to have you," she corrects, walking to Celia's side. "It's not every day our family gets bigger, but I suppose now it's finally complete."

It's like the air gets sucked out of the room. "What?" I whisper.

Callum's hand is still holding mine, I realize, and he squeezes lightly. "We haven't had that conversation yet," he says lowly, looking at his sister-by-fate.

"Why the hell not?" Chase asks from the couch, not bothering to stand.

Callum doesn't get a chance to respond, because Celia is looking at me intently. "As Callum's mate, you're one of us now. And we're happy you're here. We've been waiting a long time."

I'm frozen in my spot. His mate. Callum's mate.

They think I'm Callum's mate. And he's not disputing it. Which means...

I pull my hand from his, and he lets me go. I turn back to the door and run.

Chapter Eleven

Callum

Everything in me tells me to chase her, to comfort her, to reassure her. But I can't chase her down. I can't scare her like that.

I ball my fists and close my eyes, trying to steady myself. I take a deep, deep draw of air, and I can still smell her. I know where she is. She's scared, and she's unsettled, but she's safe.

"What the fuck?" I hiss, opening my eyes, looking at my family, all of whom are watching me with raised eyebrows.

"Why didn't you tell her?" Mae asks, looking just as mad as I feel right now.

"Because it's a big fucking deal, and she has a lot on her plate right now," I snarl, then take a deep breath, because starting a fight with the family is never a good call.

"And you didn't think, hi, I'm the one person in the world who will always treasure you, support you, love you was a good opening line?" Bethany asks.

"She was raped," I say, my voice getting very quiet, but the room goes so still that I know they all hear me. "She hasn't said it but I know she was. I could smell it and I just know. And they'd cut pieces from her. Every day. They'd take her eyes, left her blind for almost two hundred years. They'd cut her liver or her spleen and take a rib or a finger and just carve her up. Unending supply of divine halfling ingredients. And she was so young, still mortal, when all that started. So no, I don't think the information would be entirely welcome right now."

The room is silent, but Celia, being Celia, breaks the silence first. Celia is the most decisive person I know. I suppose she'd have to be. If she sees a problem, she breaks it apart, delegates the pieces, and gets it solved. Every time, for almost a thousand years.

"Well then, you'll have to convince her that you mean it then," she says. "Show her what being a mate means."

Heath sighs, and I look over to him. His eyes are sympathetic, and I know he's the only one who saw that place, who might understand right now. "She's been through some shit. That place..."

Chase squeezes Heath's thigh. "Then we'll be there." He turns to me. "But you won't start this by keeping secrets. Go tell her the truth. Now."

I nod, hoping she's had enough time that it won't feel like I'm aggressively chasing her down. She's not running, at least. She seems to have found a place to settle, and I make my way out of the house and slowly make my way there.

My heart skips half a beat when I realize she's sitting up in the tree that's in the yard of my home. Our home.

She's climbed up the tree, and I want to follow her, but she's clearly gone up there for a reason. Instead, I sit at the base of the tree. "I didn't want you to find out that way," I say, which sounds weak even to my ears.

She's silent for a long, long moment. But I wait her out. I can't do anything else. I just need to prove myself to her.

"How did you want me to find out?" she asks after an endless moment.

It's a fair enough question, and I hadn't exactly thought through it. I hadn't planned a grand gesture or anything. I wouldn't know how to.

Truth be told, all the imaginings I'd let myself have last night had been about the after, not the telling. Maybe I just thought we'd get to a place where she'd just know. That she'd be comfortable, and we'd fall in love, and we'd both know.

"I wanted you to be comfortable first," I tell her, which isn't a good answer. But it's the best I have.

She seems to consider that for a long moment. "But you were going to tell me?"

50

"Yes."

"I thought for a minute that maybe you weren't. That you weren't going to tell me."

I frown. "Why would I do that?"

I hear a rustling above me but studiously don't look up. Maybe she'll open up more if I give her as much space as I can. "I can't be what you envisioned for a mate. I figured you regretted it and were trying to forget."

My mouth goes dry with the horror just the idea brings to me. "I could never regret you." I itch to climb up there, to pull her into my arms, to make that promise a thousand times over. But I refrain.

Not the least of my reasons being that I'm not sure that the branches as high up as she is could support my weight.

"Am I what you envisioned for a mate?" she challenges.

For one brief flash of a second, I regret that my mate isn't a wolf. But only because a wolf would understand the absurdity of the question. A wolf would understand that you dream of your mate, long for your mate. Hope for your mate. Wait for them. And you dream up a million things. Fantasies. Hopes. Wishes. That your potential mate is probably always in the back of your mind. But there's never a point where I envisioned my mate. I didn't think of what I wanted them to look like, or act like. My wolf would know when it was time. And the wolves always pick correctly.

My wolf is no different than any other. She's my mate. I was made for her. Sitting on the cold ground underneath a tree is exactly where I'm meant to be right this second. I have no doubt at all.

But Marielle isn't a wolf. She doesn't have a wolf inside her, guiding her in these things. She won't understand.

"You're perfect," I tell her, completely honestly. "Marielle. You are my mate. I regret not telling you immediately, if that's what led to you thinking I don't want you. I couldn't be more proud to say I'm your mate."

There's a rustling, and then Marielle lands in a crouch in front of me, having jumped down from the tree. Her red hair is a little wild, presumably from tree branches, and I ache to push it off her face for her. I keep my hands to myself.

She tilts her head, looking at me. "What's there to be proud of?" she asks, but doesn't give me time to explain. "Callum. You know what happened to me there, right?"

I swallow. "Yes," I admit.

"It wasn't just the cutting. It was..."

She trails off, and I wonder if I should finish the thought for her. If saying *they raped you* would help or hurt.

"I was already damaged goods," she says quietly after a long moment. "I guess they thought they shouldn't waste me."

"You're not damaged goods," I say automatically, fiercely. And if I hear anyone say to her that she is, I'll fucking end them for it.

She's not looking at me again, and I fight carefully to keep control so if she does look at me, I won't scare her.

"I won't ever touch you without your consent," I tell her roughly. "I won't lay a finger on you. Not to hurt you, ever."

She nods, but still doesn't look at me. Instead, she slides from her crouch so she's sitting on her ass. She trails her hands along the ground, no doubt magically feeling so much growing beneath the soil that I'll never know about, but then wraps her arms around herself again, like she needs to protect herself.

"I wish I could be what you want," she says, and she sounds genuinely torn up about it, like what I want is somehow a primary concern here.

A wolf would understand that what I want is for her to be happy and healthy, and nothing else besides that matters. But I need to spell it out for her. "You are what I want. Exactly as you are. However that is. No expectations."

She looks at me for a brief second, as if weighing my honesty, then looks away again. "I don't know how to do this."

She was sixteen when she ended up there. She was mortal, and young, and hasn't had a moment's rest since. I'm not exactly surprised to hear that.

"However you want to do this is how to do this," I say. "I promise you, Marielle."

"Why are you being so patient?" she asks me, looking up to see me again. I bite my tongue so I don't ask, as opposed to what, exactly? Forcing myself on her?

Because yes, that is exactly what she means. And only time will convince her that will never happen again.

"You're my mate, Marielle. Whatever you need, whatever you want—I'm happy to provide it." I draw in a deep breath, not wanting to push, but needing to know. "Is this okay?"

She's still for a long moment, but then she nods, and something inside me relaxes.

We'll figure it out. Of that, I'm sure.

CHAPTER TWELVE

MARIELLE

Callum is good to his word.

I've never met a man like that before. Never met a man who keeps his word, or who has other's best interests at heart. The closest I ever got was Theo, and he never could keep his word, not when my father's will had to override everything.

But Callum is different. He shows me the house I'll live in with him, and the bedroom that is just mine. The door locks, but only from the inside. I'm sure the lock isn't enough to keep a wolf out if they really want in, but it's the principle of the matter.

It's a nice room. The bed feels like a cloud, and there's a huge window that overlooks the valley, with a good view of a currently flowering tree outside. All the clothes Honor brought me are in the closet, along with too many others. They're more than one person could possibly every need, and in so many different styles.

It's not just things they've provided me, either. After two days of meandering around Callum's house and letting him take me on walks around our yard and wondering what I'm possibly going to do with my life, Celia knocks on Callum's front door at eight in the morning and invites herself to breakfast.

She gives her brother a rather unimpressed look, leaning against his kitchen counter. "You have a job, Callum."

He sputters over the coffee he's been drinking. "You let Bryce go off for three years!"

It's easy to see why Celia is a queen. Her look doesn't waver, not even for a second, and Callum eventually grumbles but leaves the room to change his clothes. He returns in a fresh set of clothes with a sword strapped to his side. "I'll be back later," he tells me. "And if you need anything, ask anyone. They'll find me for you."

Celia watches him go without saying another word, waiting until the door clicks shut. "There we go," she says, and some of the stiffness in her posture relaxes, like she can release the commanding presence. "I thought you might want a break from him."

Did I? I'm honestly not sure.

She continues on. "I know the mating bond can be intense, and since your kind don't even properly feel it, and considering everything... well, I thought I'd kill two birds with one stone. You get a break, and I get to talk to you without Callum breathing down my neck."

I take a deep breath. That sounds ominous. What could she want to talk to me about that she doesn't want Callum to hear?

"My siblings don't think I remember, because it's been so long, but I remember the early days after Bethany and I mated. It's a lot. No shame if you need a break from him." She looks at me sideways. "And no shame if you want to talk to people who aren't him about certain things. I might not be your first choice for everything, I know I'm..." She gestures to herself, as if that gesture encompasses all of who she is. "But I thought I'd offer. Anything you want to talk about that you don't want to talk to him about. I imagine you have questions."

Do I have questions? Yes, like how the hell phones work and what makes cars go. And what exactly is going on with clothes today, and how sometimes people say things so beyond my comprehension. But what I ask is, "You've been mated to Bethany for a long time?"

She looks at me like she expected me to ask this. "Almost my whole life. What do you want to know about mating?"

"What does it mean? How does it work?" I ask her.

She stops to consider it for just a second, although I get the feeling that she has an answer ready. She's just trying to put it in terms I, a non-wolf, will understand. "It's a fated bond," she says. "Fate drives you to someone who will complete you. Equal you, give you every happiness. And the moment the wolf meets their mate, that's it. They know."

"That's all it takes?"

She shrugs. "You're his mate forever now, and he'll always know that. But to cement the bond, to accept it and make it permanent, if you wanted, you'll let him bite you. Under the full moon."

I flush, already knowing what that would entail.

She sees my flush and smiles a bit. "Bite him back," she advises, like it's a foregone conclusion that Callum and I will get there. Maybe it is for the wolves. "Trust me."

That makes me flush even more, just thinking about it.

"How are you liking our town?" Celia asks, evidently completely unaware of the turmoil I'm feeling.

"It's great," I say. And it is great. But I would never say anything else, even if it weren't great.

"You've seen very little of it, though, right?" Celia presses, but it's clear she doesn't need my answer. She sighs, running a hand through her hair. "I'll talk to Callum. Wolves can be a little territorial when we first mate. But I'll remind him that there's more to life than him."

How am I meant to respond to that? The truth is, I like Callum, because he's treated me well. And I don't know what to do in a town among so many strangers.

But if I'm going to be here—maybe forever—I should learn. This is my home now, as Callum's reminded me a dozen times already.

"Alright."

"Good." She seems pleased, genuinely pleased, even giving me a small smile. "Now, tell me about you. What do you like? What are you hoping to find here?"

Find here? Safety, I suppose, but I don't think that's the right answer.

But suddenly I know the answer. "Do you need an herbalist?" I ask. "I'm good at that, especially medicine."

Celia nods. "That could work. Come with me."

I follow her, but she stops when we go to leave the house. "It's cold here," she says, although I notice she's not wearing a jacket. She takes the jacket off the hook by the door and hands it to me.

"This isn't mine."

Her smile returns. "Trust me. Callum won't be offended."

The jacket dwarfs me, but it feels so nice around me. Smells nice, too, clean and like the forest surrounding us. I zip it around me, letting it surround me.

"We have two major needs for medicine," Celia tells me as we walk. "One, obviously, children. I'll never understand all the ways they find to hurt themselves. Wolf children rarely get sick, but when they do, it's bad. Every parent here would thank you forever if you could spare their children even a bit of that."

I nod. "And what's the other need?"

She stops, then nods her head ahead. "These idiots."

I turn to look, and I see wolves lunging at each other, fights breaking out left, right, and center. I tense to turn and run, but then realize that Celia hasn't done anything to break up the fights.

"Callum's soldiers," she explains. "They're fully grown, obviously, so their injuries heal. But if you could do anything to spare them the pain of healing, and anyways, sometimes they bite off more than they can chew. Think they're more invulnerable than they actually are."

I watch the clashes with a new light. Training exercises. Alright.

I don't see Callum in the crowd, but I do see Honor, approaching another wolf with a ferocious speed I wouldn't expect if I wasn't seeing it with my own eyes.

I can see what Celia means, about some of them getting in over their head.

"I'll do it," I say.

She smiles at me. "Excellent. Let's go to my office—I want a list of everything you'll need, alright?"

CHAPTER THIRTEEN

CALLUM

Celia keeps forcing me to go to work.

Bryce got three years essentially uninterrupted after meeting Mae, but I get sent back to work days after.

But Celia's probably not wrong. Marielle isn't like Mae. Marielle twitches if she's touched accidentally and has nightmares most nights, and Celia is probably right to make me give her some space. The wolf in me insists we can comfort her, heal her. The wolf in me is probably wrong.

So I go to work. I keep up my physical strength and training, and if I work the soldiers harder than I usually do, they have the good sense not to complain.

Five days after I'm sent back to work, Celia and Marielle walk onto the training grounds. Each of them is carrying a box, and Celia walks them both right over to the table set up on the far end.

I realize as they get a little closer that Marielle is wearing my coat, and that sends a jolt of warmth through me. My scent on her skin. Does she like that?

I drop what I'm doing and jog over to them. "Marielle, hi. What's up?"

Celia speaks first. "Marielle has offered to put her herbalist skills to use and heal you idiots when you play too rough."

I watch her. She doesn't look at me, too busy going through the boxes she and Celia set down on the table, no doubt full of her supplies.

"Thank you."

She looks up at that and gives me a small smile, which, as always, makes my heart contract. "Happy to help. I've missed things like this. Send anyone who needs me my way, please."

"Will do."

Celia clears her throat. "They're waiting for you, Callum."

I want to snap that they can wait all damn day. Call it an exercise in patience. Or they can just carry on without me.

But Marielle, still wearing my damned jacket, is setting up bottles and tins, biting her lip as she thinks, and I know Celia is right. The best thing to do is leave her to it, so I nod.

Celia walks back out with me. "Joining us for a fight today?" I know she doesn't get to train as often as she'd like, as busy as she is.

"Don't I wish. No, I have business."

"I appreciate you making time for Marielle."

"I always will. She's my sister now, you know. And believe me, I could use more sisters."

Indeed. We used to joke that Celia found Bethany so young because the fates knew Celia was sick and tired of just us three brothers for company.

She stops me with a hand on my arm. "Be careful with her, alright? She's settling in. She can be happy here, I can feel it. Let her figure it out."

I swallow. "Of course." Always. Whatever she needs.

Celia nods, releases my arm, and leaves.

***

There are better places to station an herbalist than the training grounds, but Celia knows exactly what she's doing.

I question for about half a second if this will scare Marielle, but no. I feel her eyes on me almost constantly.

It takes about an hour before I can't stand it anymore, before the constant awareness of her looking at me wins. The wolf in me is howling to go to her, to focus solely on her. And I can't fight it anymore.

I turn so she hopefully can't see what I'm doing and cut my hand open on my knife.

Jake gives me a very unimpressed look. "Think she'll fall for that?"

I snap half-heartedly at him. Probably not, honestly. But I don't have much time before the wound heals over on its own, so if I want to see her, it has to be now.

I jog over to her table. She has a chair now, and she sits there with dozens of glass containers in front of her. There's not a label in sight, but I suppose as a druid she doesn't really need one.

"What can I do for you?" she asks, and she smiles at me again, and it's like everything inside me is lit on fire at the sight.

I've started making a list of what makes her smile, determined to give it to her always. And maybe I'm wrong, but I think I just made her smile.

"My hand," I blurt out, holding it out to her. "I cut it."

It's a weak excuse and we both know it. It'll be healed in five more minutes, if that. But she takes my outstretched hand anyway, and I thrill a little at the contact.

She plucks a flower off the table and holds it to my skin. To me, it looks like a weed, one of the thousands that grows around here, but I don't question her. She knows way more about it than I do, after all.

She covers it with her own hand, using the other hand to cradle mine, and I hold perfectly still. I don't even breathe.

After a moment, she pulls her hand and the flower away, although she keeps cradling my hand. I blink. "It's gone."

The cut is gone, like it was never there. I don't know what I expected. But I never knew a flower could do this.

She gives me a smile again, a shy one this time. "It's like what I did with the tree the night we met," she explains. "Transferring the energy. I can't do this every time, and it's more dependable to make proper treatments. But this one was easy."

"That's impressive," I say. She still hasn't dropped my hand. I worry if I say anything too loud, she'll realize.

She shrugs. "It's what I do. And I'm happy to help." She drops my hand then, but I don't think I imagine that she squeezes it before she does. "Be careful out there, alright?"

I nod, and, half in a daze, turn back to the training ground.

My hand won't stop tingling from her touch for the rest of the day.

CHAPTER FOURTEEN

MARIELLE

M ae talks to me about clothes. She seems to always dress like she did on the
day I met her, wearing clothes I gather are still more than a little daring,
even in this modern day. All of her clothes expose miles of skin, and every single
piece seems to be black. She's very short, but makes up for it a bit with shoes that
I don't understand how she walks in. But even with the platform boots she wears
most often, she's still short compared to the Crae siblings.

She shows me pictures of what people wear and explains things, and just
accepts the choices I make without judgment. I don't end up with clothes like
hers, even as I'm sure she'd be happy to help me dress that way.

Mostly I end up with the leggings Honor brought me, or jeans. Trousers are
a wonderful idea, although I took some skirts. I'm just used to them.

Chase and Mae are both casters and have taken me in as a member of their
little caster club. Apparently there are precious few of us up here, in the wolf
village, so they stick close together.

On a particularly chilly morning a few weeks after I arrive in the village, the
three of us take a walk outside. It's nice, like a little club of not only casters but
also outsiders, mates who have joined this family and view it from an outside
perspective. But both Mae and Chase are more than happy to be here and never

have a negative word to say about the village. If anything, they're doing more to talk it up to me than anyone else is.

The chill hasn't left the air, and when I left our house that morning, I took Callum's jacket again, feeling him watch me the entire time. But he doesn't stop me.

I'm drowning in Callum's coat, but neither Mae nor Chase look in any way bothered by the cold, wearing their usual clothes.

For Mae, that means fishnet stockings that do nothing to protect from the cold, a short skirt, most of her midriff and most of her arms exposed. "How are you not freezing?" I ask her.

She shrugs. "Heat spells. Work them into the fabric."

Chase snorts. "A perfectly good waste of magic, if you ask me."

She points a finger in his face, but I can tell this is a well-worn conversation, not a real argument. I'm starting to get good at recognizing those in the family here. "First off, witches can't waste magic like you can, so stuff it. Second of all, I don't take advice about weather-related clothing choices from a man whose internal body temperature is a hundred and ten degrees."

I blink at him. "Really?"

Chase shrugs. "Demon, remember? It's hot in Demonheim. We're built for it." He turns back to Mae. "It's frivolous magic, anyways."

She shrugs. "Witches are allowed to be frivolous."

From what I've gathered, Mae's magic is mostly about intent. It's about gathering what she wants and pouring intent into it, and waiting, and then seeing what she wants emerging.

Chase's magic is different. It takes energy, and it's not always his. He'd explained that old human myths about demons making deals with humans aren't entirely inaccurate, because that is a way to get energy. But one of the reasons demons have mates like wolves do is a mate is an unending source of energy, a give-and-take.

Every time he talks about his magic, it sounds like contracts and agreements and rules. I could never understand magic like that. But he's comfortable with it, and I don't ask too much.

For me, being outside is the purest thing I've felt in two hundred years. Every time we walk, I can feel the grass beneath my feet, the trees blooming around us, the flowers pushing their way to the sun. It's magical and invigorating.

Bryce is waiting for us when we circle past the house he shares with Mae when they're in the village. Callum made it sound like they're never here, but they haven't left since I arrived. "You're late," he tells her, raising an eyebrow and crossing his arms, but he can't stop the small smile that changes his grumpy expression.

"I'm never late, you're just early," Mae tells him, smiling. She walks towards him, but then turns to Chase and I. "Staying for stabbing practice?"

Chase rolls his eyes. "I'm perfectly skilled at stabbing, thank you. And no," he says, the moment Mae opens her mouth, "that was not innuendo. Besides," he continues, turning his head towards his own home, "I'm working today."

Mae cackles. "Little incubus action?"

Chase just rolls his eyes. "Shut the fuck up. Real work."

"Why are you demeaning the hard work of incubi everywhere? Sex demons work hard too, you know."

"Who's a sex demon?" Heath says, walking over from his and Chase's home.

Chase's lip quirks. "Me, apparently. And if you don't know that after four centuries..."

"Never doubted you for a second," Heath says, breezing over. He looks Chase up and down, as if drinking him in, and reaches out to take his hands. "You leaving soon?"

"Right now."

"Just came to say goodbye then."

Chase leans in and kisses him, slow and sweet. "Call me back for dinner," he murmurs, untangling his hands from Heath's and then disappearing.

I blink at where he once was, staring.

"Demon magic," Heath says to me.

I swallow. I'll never properly understand the terms of demon magic, but I'm getting acquainted with it quickly, evidently. "What does he mean, call him back for dinner?" I ask, turning to face Heath instead of the spot his mate just vanished from.

He shrugs. "Demon magic is all about energy exchanges. It relies on pretty strict rules. Like demon bargains that the humans talk about. Traveling that way takes a lot of energy. So to save energy, I can make a deal to call him back, and use my energy. Which is basically penalty free, because I'm his mate; the rules are complex. Anyways, the oldest form of demon bargain is just knowing a demon's true name. You call Chase's true name with intention, you're offering your energy, and he'll come to you."

"Oh," I say, trying to understand the rules.

All my magic requires is me to feel the thrum and energy of the earth. Chase's makes my head spin.

Heath quirks a small smile. "It's Chase Crae," he says, startling me. "If that's what you were wondering."

"I wasn't." But my throat feels tighter. Knowing a demon's true name, such an evidently powerful talisman...

Why would I ever be given this?

Heath's eyes suddenly become intense. "He'd want you to know," he says. "But understand, the only people who do know to call him that, who can make that demon bargain, are the seven of us, and his king and queen. And I'm not even sure the demon king and queen have tried since Chase Crae became his true name. So it's not something you spread around, get me?"

I don't think Heath would ever hurt me, but the intensity in his eyes tells me he'll do anything to protect his mate. I nod, hesitantly.

As soon as I nod, Heath smiles. It makes the scar through his eye twist, so he doesn't really look less intimidating, but there's a softness in his smile that makes me think there's genuine affection under there. "Good," he says, then looks over to where Bryce and Mae are. "Are you joining the lesson?"

"What is the lesson?"

"Knives," Bryce says, apparently having been listening the whole time.

Mae turns and grins. "My darling mate is worried I rely too much on magic and wants to make sure I can defend myself even if I can't cast an enchantment."

Bryce rolls his eyes. "So you enchanted the shit out of your knives. Defeating the whole point."

Mae shrugs, revealing two wickedly sharp knives. "Witches gonna witch. Can't blame me."

Bryce doesn't retort, just looking at her fondly.

Bryce turns his attention back to me, although I have a feeling he's still half-watching Mae. "Will you be joining us?"

I swallow, still watching Mae's knives, remembering the feeling of a knife in my hand, so long ago. I doubt it's something you can forget.

"Have any to lend me?" I ask, and Bryce, who usually perpetually looks a little grumpy, grins.

Chapter Fifteen

Callum

When she's not back when I'd expect her to be, I take a deep breath, scent the air, and follow Marielle's scent outside.

She's usually back long before the time we leave for the training ground, but time is ticking by and I haven't seen her.

I don't want to crowd her, but I'm still a little jumpy when she's out of my sight. My wolf very well knows she's been hurt, and doesn't understand why protecting her from inside the den isn't a feasible solution.

But I've been so proud of her, so happy to see her making connections. She walks with Mae and Chase most mornings these past few weeks, and eats dinner with the whole family every night. She comes to the training ground every day I've trained, and has even gone to quite a few homes to help treat children for their youthful injuries. She talks to everyone at least a little.

I can see that sometimes she's forcing it, pushing herself. But other times she seems to genuinely enjoy my family, and I just hope it's a sign that some part of her is starting to know she's safe here.

And other times, when the others aren't around, we've been making connections, too.

It's just little things, and every little thing makes my heart soar. She smiles at me more and more frequently. We read together on the couch in the evening. She even watches TV with me sometimes now, although I can tell she mostly prefers the quiet of books. Which is more than fine by me; she tucks her legs up onto the couch when she reads, and one time, her foot brushed my thigh.

The good part of me thought of a future where she'd be comfortable enough to shove her feet under my thighs. I don't even care if they're cold. Or maybe drape them across my lap, letting me rub them and her calves for her while she relaxes.

The less-good part of me thought about grabbing her foot, starting kisses at her ankle bone and working my way up, slowly, torturously slowly, until she begs for my head between her thighs.

That had carried over to my dreams that night. Which isn't unusual. I don't know a wolf alive who doesn't fantasize about giving head to their mate. It's animalistic and sloppy, full of smells and tastes unique to your mate. I've had this dream a thousand times before.

But now there is a face. A body. A voice. A scent. Now I wake up aching, harder than I ever thought it would be possible to be.

Now I can't push the thought to the back of my mind.

I jerk off more than I ever have in my entire life.

And then I see her again. Always innocent little moments, and I know she has no idea what she does to me. A smile. A question, and the little tilt to her head that accompanies it. The way her lips move when she eats, when she talks. And I'm hard all over again.

What would she look like with my head between her thighs?

What would her cunt taste like?

I have to stop myself there. I haven't tasted her lips yet. She's not ready for any of this. She made that perfectly clear the day she found out she was my mate.

And I respect that. Every smile feels like a gift, like a treasure I worked for. And I'll work every day for the rest of my existence to earn whatever she's ready to give me.

So with that in mind, I go outside to find her, following her delicious scent.

She's outside Bryce and Mae's home, and I realize belatedly that a lot of my family is with her.

Bryce is putting her through her paces with knife work, and it's only a thousand years of brotherhood that stops me from snarling and lunging. That, and the fact that she's keeping up with him.

She's fast. Where Bryce, as big and strong as I am, as any wolf is, dominates the fight in sheer physical aggression, she moves around him, dodging underneath his arms, and often getting behind him before he can catch up.

Not sporting, but wolves aren't particularly known for fighting fair, either.

I watch, my feet frozen to the ground, as she weaves under his arm and tags him between his shoulder blades. Blood hits the air, but she barely knicks him and the wound will be healed in a few minutes.

Bryce breathes deeply, smiling for once, and turns to her. "You know what you're doing."

She immediately hands the blade to him, hilt out, and he looks at it for a long moment before he accepts it back.

Good. If my mate likes knives, she'll have a dozen. But they won't be Bryce's cast-offs. They'll be made for her, and I'll provide them.

"Where'd you learn that, Marielle?" Mae asks, arms crossed from where she's standing off to the side.

Marielle shrugs, self-consciousness returning. I ache to ease it, if only I knew how.

"I had a brother," Marielle says, and her voice is quiet, but I'm so attuned to it now I think I could hear it anywhere. "He made sure I knew how to defend myself, whenever we had a moment."

I think of Chase, who's out on a mission now to find anything he can about her family, about the father and this brother. Maybe her mother too, if he can. My mate has been out of the world for two hundred years; it's time she knew what was out there still.

The brother was a human. He must be gone by now; their lifespans are practically a blink. But I think she'd at least like to know anything she can. His final resting place, maybe.

Heath smiles from over near Mae. "Well, he taught you well."

"I'm just glad I remembered it," she says.

"Like riding a bike," Heath dismisses. "Right, Callum?"

Called out for my staring, I approach. "Beautiful, Marielle."

Her brow furrows. "Stabbing your brother?"

Bryce barks out a laugh, and I still startle a little at that. He's not a miserable man, but he wasn't much prone to laughter. Not before Mae, at any rate. "Oh, little halfling, don't oversell it. You scratched me."

The furrow between her eyes doesn't lessen. "I could've stabbed you."

"Of that I don't doubt," I say, before Bryce can say something stupid back, like saying—honestly—if he let his wolf have more control, she never would have stood a chance.

But still, the way she moved...

I've been at war my whole life. I know fighting; I know weapons. And Marielle has all the makings of greatness, if she wants that.

Heath clears his throat, and I realize how intensely I've been staring at her. "We hijacked Mae's lesson," he points out.

Mae groans theatrically. "You had to remind him."

I walk closer, and Marielle both holds her ground and her eye contact. I force myself to hide a smile of victory. "Would you like to take a walk, Marielle?"

And there it is. Her smile again, soft and so sweet. Delicate, almost like it's afraid to come out. But she's somehow brave enough to do it anyway.

I'm going to lay the world at this woman's feet. Just wait and see.

***

She actually takes my hand as I extend mine to her, and we walk along the tree line, away from Mae's lesson.

"That was beautiful," I tell her again.

"Do wolves find fighting beautiful?" she asks.

I shrug. "I suppose it depends on the fighter. You move so gracefully. I can't help it. You should train with us. Well. Not with us, if you don't want it," remembering belatedly how violent the clash of my soldiers can look. "But since you're there, you could strengthen these skills further. You should join us."

"I was worried I'd forgotten," she admits softly. "It's been a while."

70

I hesitate, not wanting to seem insensitive, but... "If your brother taught you that, then how..."

"How'd I get captured," she finishes flatly.

I hesitate, but nod. There's no good way to ask the question.

She doesn't look at me as she answers, but she does answer. I hope it's a sign of trust. I worry she thinks she has to.

"Mostly because I was surprised," she says evenly. "And outnumbered. Theo taught me how to use a blade to defend myself, but don't think—druids have defensive magic too. But I..." She hesitates, and it seems painful, and part of me wants to tell her to stop, to not worry. But part of me needs to know. "My father was in on it."

I stop dead in my tracks, which has the unfortunate outcome of my dead-weight yanking on her hand when she keeps walking, but I can't help myself. "What?"

CHAPTER SIXTEEN

MARIELLE

I didn't realize he'd be so surprised by that revelation. When he yanks on my hand, I stop and turn to face him, but I can't quite meet his eyes.

I don't know why. Maybe I don't know what I'll see there.

He's already danced around calling me weak and helpless in the last few minutes. This story might push him a little further in his thinking.

I always knew I'd prove I wasn't worth thinking about as a mate, that fate had screwed him over when it came to me.

"Marielle, what did he do to you?" he asks, and his voice is deeper than I ever heard it. There's a rumble under it that makes me shiver.

"He told me right before it happened that he owed them a debt. Now I know it was probably over an enslavement spell. Maybe he was trying to replace Theo. I don't know. But he did what any competent druid would do. He drugged me. We'd made a thousand of those drugs, I should have known. I just didn't expect it. I woke up with the shackle already on, and warlocks on their way to collect me."

The rumble becomes a full-on growl, and I automatically step back.

He freezes. "Never have to be afraid of me," he mutters.

I look down. I haven't dropped his hand yet. "I'm not." It's not entirely true.

But it's not entirely a lie, either. Everything scares me. He scares me. But he also comforts me.

"The wolf in me aches to protect his mate," he explains. His voice is still rougher than I'm used to, but the growling's stopped. "It wants to rip out throats for you, Marielle. It will never hurt you."

Well, that's... something.

Rip out throats for me?

He's already done it, a part of me whispers. Nothing in that manor I was kept in survived.

Would he rip out my father's throat?

Do I want him to?

Aches to protect his mate. Who has ever wanted to protect me before?

"Do you believe me, Marielle?" he asks, voice deep and rumbly still, but so earnest, like he'll be crestfallen if I truly ever believed he'd hurt me.

"I do. I know you'll never hurt me."

"No one will ever hurt you again," he says, ferocity creeping into his tone, but the rumbling is easing out of his voice. And then, bizarrely, a smile creeps onto his face. "But I think my mate can protect herself, hm?" His thumb starts tracing patterns on the back of the hand he's still holding. "I'll get you the finest blades you've ever seen."

I can't stop from smiling, but flick my free hand, bringing a tree root from the ground under our feet to the surface. "I don't need knives to protect myself."

His eyes gleam. "No," he agrees. "Not when the very earth will rise to your defense."

He says it like he's proud of the fact, like he enjoys it, and I can't help but smile back even wider.

Chapter Seventeen

Marielle

The next day, when we walk over to the training ground, Callum steers me away from my table and towards a spot on the actual grounds.

"I borrowed some knives for you," he says. "They're Honor's, but she says you can use them until we can get you your own. I want to see what you can do."

I swallow nervously, but accept the knives. I can do this, I know I can. I doubt I'm actually a match for a fully trained werewolf, but I also know Callum won't let things get out of hand.

So why am I nervous? Is it that Callum is watching?

Jake steps forward. "Alright, Marielle," Callum says. "Put him on the ground."

That I can do without the knives. Jake takes half a step forward. I wait for the moment where his balance is weakest, and lash his leg with a tree root.

It knocks him to the ground, and for good measure, I have the tree root pin him in place by that ankle, so he can't lunge up for more.

Jakes goes down with barely more than a grunt, but when it's over, he watches me with some sort of weary respect in his eyes.

Callum, by contrast, looks at me in a way that feels hungry. I shiver under it, but I don't think I dislike it.

"And with just the knives?" he asks, then spares half a glance at Jake before looking right back at me. "He'll stick to just the knives too." There's an underlying threat in his voice, but I don't even have to look at Jake to know Callum will be obeyed.

I let Jake go, and he springs back up, grinning. "Badass," he murmurs, lining himself back up to try again.

We go four more times. Jake gets me more often than I get him, but it feels good to figure out his strategies, and to start adapting to them.

I could have kept going for another hour, maybe two, but then someone comes over to Callum with a bloody gash across his forearm. I break away to look at it and treat it, and I realize as I disengage from Jake that something in Callum's shoulders relaxes.

The cut isn't hard to treat, not with the wolf's healing already at work, so I send him on his way soon enough.

"Want to see somewhere beautiful?" Callum asks me suddenly.

"What do you want to show me?" I ask, looking around the training field.

He smiles widely. "You'll see." He turns to the others, raising his voice. "You're done for the day, go home!"

There're intermittent cheers, and then Callum leads me away from the crowd.

So I follow him. He could be taking me somewhere awful, I suppose, although he's gone to a lot of effort to keep me safe for me to actually think that. But I follow him, and I don't ask.

We go past the town center, where I really haven't gone that often yet. At least, not during the busy parts of the day. But we don't stop there either.

"You good to walk a while?" he asks as we reach the hills on the far side of the valley. "I know that was a lot today already."

I could walk all day. A human's muscles might atrophy to nothing after captivity, but not mine. I feel like I have more energy now. I could walk—and run and fight and everything else—all day.

"I'm ready," I say.

His smile always startles me. It makes his face look beautiful, wide and open, but that's not why it sticks out to me so much.

I think I'm just unused to seeing people smile.

So we walk, the air around us growing quieter as we go. I've noticed that there aren't many wild animals near here. Maybe they can tell that the village is full of predators.

But while I might not hear animals, the trees and flowers and grasses whisper to me, caressing me. Welcoming me home.

Home.

Finally, he draws to a stop, gesturing to a clearing up ahead. It's only now that I realize that it's gotten louder again, although not with animals or wolves or anyone else.

"Come see," he invites me, and extends a hand to me.

I don't even hesitate, taking it in mine, and he stares at it for just a moment, another smile breaking over his face, before he clasps my fingers in his warm hand and leads me to the waterfall spilling over the edge of the mountain.

The roar is a deafening cascade around us, the water disappearing into the ground below. I didn't realize how high we climbed, how far the valley below us is, but it's as if we're on the top of the world.

Wolf ears can probably hear over the waterfall, but I barely can, so I don't try to talk. But I do squeeze the hand still holding mine, and I hope he understands.

CHAPTER EIGHTEEN

CALLUM

E very single smile feels like a shot of adrenaline, like I just won a battle, like everything is slotting into place. I ride high on them for the rest of the day.

Not even when my brothers and Chase corner me at dinner can my elation be dimmed.

I'm making progress. It's slow progress, but it's progress at her pace, and it's all I want in the entire damn world.

"You thought of what you'll do this weekend?" Bryce asks me first.

This weekend, and the oncoming full moon, just three days away.

I can't be here. Can't be around her.

While wolves only ever fully transform as a response to great emotional distress or trauma, we can control aspects of the shift most of the time. Those of us who train our wolf natures can call forth strength and claws and fangs, and use those traits to our advantage.

But on the full moon, it's not optional. We have claws and fangs, and our minds go a little feral. And those of us with mates...

We rut. Like animals, basically.

From what I know, it's usually an immensely enjoyable experience. Ecstasy, really, if both parties are on board.

Marielle is not ready for that.

I level my eyes with Chase. "Need a favor."

He huffs. "You're racking them up here, Callum."

"You know I'm good for it." That reminds me, though, that I need to strike a demon bargain with him. While he's hunting down Marielle's past, he can kill her father on sight. I'll gladly pay any amount of energy the demon demands for that.

And Chase'll enjoy the hell out of it, too.

"What do you need?"

"Do you think you could go to Demonheim and convince Ryder to lock me up?"

Heath sucks in a breath. "You sure?"

I shrug. "It'd be effective." No one escapes Demonheim. Save Heath, of course. But for one single night? Even strong and nearly feral with the moon, I wouldn't have a chance.

Being in a separate plane of existence from Marielle is the only way I can think of to protect her. I won't be able to scent her, won't be able to reach her. I'll be out of my mind with wanting, and she won't be any the wiser.

"It's not a place where you want to be locked up."

"They'd let him out when the moon is past," Chase points out. Then he brightens. "Hey. If I can get Ryder to agree to look after your sorry ass, maybe Hannah will come here? Keep Marielle company while everyone is busy."

And Marielle can meet the only other halfling we know. Perfect.

Heath's eyes are still intense, though. "Callum. Are you sure? You'll do this every month? For as long as she needs?"

Am I sure? She needs this. She needs us to be slow. That's all I ever needed to hear. "Whatever she needs."

Bryce nods slowly, elbowing Heath in the side. "You wouldn't say any different."

Heath opens his mouth—he probably would never ever willingly consent to being locked up in Demonheim again—but then looks at Chase and closes it. He nods. "Alright, it's a plan."

***

I tell Marielle the day before the full moon. Chase has agreed to take me over to Demonheim tonight, so we can be sure I'll be locked up far before there's any actual danger or problems, and before Chase is too busy with his own mate to worry about me. In exchange, Hannah has agreed to come spend the full moon with Marielle. I hope they get along.

She watches me for a minute, considering what I'm telling her, and I worry that I've been too truthful. That I've put too fine a point on it, that she understands how sex-crazed my wolf—and I—am for her right now.

But then again, I'm not going to lie to her. And she should know how badly I want her. As long as she also knows I'd never touch her without her permission.

"Do you get more wolf-like, closer to the moon?" she asks.

The question surprises me slightly. "Not usually," I say, thinking it over. But extreme emotions might change that. And what could be more extreme than falling in love with your mate, even as you ache to protect her, and mourn the things you couldn't protect her from? "What have you seen?"

She shrugs. "Growling and grumbling, mostly."

I probably have been doing that. "Does it bother you?" Of course it must, a wolf who towers over her has been growling, and—

She shakes her head, making her hair fan out around her face. She so often wears it braided, but has taken to leaving it down around the house, and I love to watch it bounce and move. Ache to bury my face in it. Want to breathe the scent first thing in the morning, want to run my fingers through it to soothe her back to sleep, want it to tickle my skin as I hold her.

"No," she says. "You wouldn't hurt me."

My heart stops for a moment, then starts beating faster, faster, until I'm worried it will beat out of my chest, until I'm worried she can hear it.

You won't hurt me. It's said with confidence, assurance. Have more beautiful words ever been spoken?

It's the bare minimum. She should never have any cause to doubt it, and it's the least she should ever expect of me. She should expect more, demand more—

But she didn't, even weeks ago. She didn't know she should expect it. And now she does, and that's progress.

"True," I say, and I can hear the rumble in my own voice then, the wolf close enough to the surface. "Understand this: I'll never hurt you. And the wolf would never hurt you." We're one and the same, especially in this; she is our mate, and we will die before we hurt her.

She nods. "I know. So that's why you're leaving?"

I nod. "Yeah. The wolf, when it has more control, it might not realize..." It wouldn't hurt her. Not physically.

But there are so many other ways to do damage. And she knows that well.

She looks at me for a long, long minute, and I force myself not to interrupt. I have no idea what she's thinking, and it's unnerving as she just keeps watching me.

"You'll be okay?" she asks after a long moment.

It takes me a moment to muster the ability to respond. She's worried about me? I just told her the beast inside me will gain strength and want to hunt her down, might inadvertently assault her, and she worries about me?

"I'll be fine," I say, although I can't quite say it's true. I've never been to Demonheim, but I've heard enough from Heath about the cages, and I know for a fact he never told us the half of it.

It's one night, though. And it's for Marielle. Knowing that, I could survive anything.

I would rip out my own bones, cut off my own limbs, for her. One night in the cages is negligible.

"Ryder is the king of Demonheim. And his mate, Hannah, she's a halfling like you. She's asked to come see you, while I'm there. How do you feel about it?" I ask, hoping she won't ask again about how I'll be in those cages.

She actually smiles a bit, tilting her head, intrigued. "I've never met another halfling."

"She'll be here tonight. Chase is going to do the swap soon."

She bites her lip, but nods. "And you'll be back when the moon is over?"

"I promise."

There's a knock on our front door. Chase. I need to go, need to not keep him waiting, but I hesitate. "You'll be okay, Marielle?"

She raises an eyebrow. "I'm not the one going through the full moon in a different realm."

Well, when she puts it like that...

I want to do something like hug her or kiss her. I'd settle for even just the back of her hand.

I keep my hands to myself, nod, and go to answer the door.

Chapter Nineteen

Marielle

I miss him as soon as he's gone.

It's ridiculous, but it feels like an absence, and more than it does when we're just in different locations around the village. It feels wrong.

I wrap my arms around my stomach and sink into the couch. He won't be back until after the full moon, so I need to figure out how to handle this feeling.

After about twenty minutes, Chase reappears with a tall, dark-eyed demon next to him.

No. Not a demon. She has horns, but her hair is pinned back, and I can see her pointed ears.

Hannah. The halfling. Like me.

Chase smiles as he goes towards the door. "Hannah, meet Marielle. Marielle, meet Hannah. Your cousin." Then he's gone, leaving us here together.

Hannah is tall, with intense dark eyes and a rather regal bearing. Then I remember that she's the queen of the demons, and I stand up, trying to be welcoming and gracious.

"It's been a long time since I've met another halfling," she says. Her voice is deep and even.

"I've never met one before," I tell her.

"From what I've heard, you've never had much of a chance to meet anyone."

I wince. True. And she apparently doesn't put things delicately.

I try for a welcoming smile. I'm sure it fails. "Would you like to sit down?"

She nods, settling on the couch, and I join her.

She's where Callum usually sits, and apparently not even this stranger in my home can distract my mind from thinking about him. I try to push it to the back of my mind, but it doesn't quite work.

"Chase told Ryder and I what happened to you," she says. "You can rest assured, the demons will join the werewolves in fighting back against this. If there are any more of those fucks out there, we'll find them."

"Thank you," I say, because it seems like the thing to say.

"Don't thank me. It just makes sense. Besides, to think of them holding you like that, cutting pieces from you..." she shudders. "Let's just say, Ryder realized very quickly it could have been me. And that was the end of the conversation."

Right. The demon king, protecting his mate.

"I wish we could have met under better circumstances, but I truly am glad to meet you, cousin," she continues.

"Will Callum be okay?" I blurt out, thinking of the unpleasant circumstances that have brought us here. Callum. I think part of my brain keeps thinking he's right upstairs, or outside on the training fields, and will be back in a moment. And then every time I remember that's not true, it sets off a fresh wave of a feeling I can't even properly name.

She shifts, considering. "It's not a pleasant place," she admits. "The cages, I mean. Demonheim itself is lovely. But the cages are miserable. He must really care about you."

Hot guilt settles in my gut, squirming and consuming.

"It's not long though," she continues on, not seeing my distress. "He'll recover after."

But does he plan to go back next month? Every month? How will that add up on him?

"Ryder will look after him," she adds, maybe picking up on my distress. "Don't worry, little cousin. Your mate will be fine, at the end of this."

"Are we cousins?"

She shrugs. "Who can say? Did you ever meet your divine parent?"

"No."

"Me either. Gather my dad was a love 'em and leave 'em type. If it even counted as love. And I grew up among demons, so…" She shrugs. "We could be cousins. Who could say? Do you know anything about them?"

"My mother kept me until I could be weaned," I say, remembering the story of my childhood. "And then left me to my father. Wasn't worth keeping me, apparently." Not divine enough, I'd always assumed. They say the divine have immense, awe-inspiring abilities, only a tier below their godly ancestors. And I have no such talents. I can grow plants like the best of the druids, but all I got from my mother are my pointed ears.

"Yeah, well. Me either. I'm more demon than anything else, I think. And I can't say I'm worse off for it. You ever met any of them?"

"No. You?"

She smiles softly. "Once or twice. But I'm older than you, Marielle. And I can tell you, the experience wasn't anything special."

There's something in her eyes that tells me that there's more to the experience, but I don't push. "Do you want to see the village?" I ask her instead.

She nods, so I lead her outside to show her around.

CHAPTER TWENTY

MARIELLE

T he next morning, Mae warns us not to go outside tonight.

"Why?" I ask. "Will it be dangerous?" I actually really wanted to see the moon tonight. It's full for the first time that I can see it in two centuries, and I wanted to take it in.

Mae, Hannah, and I are out on our normal morning walk. Chase has elected to stay in with Heath, and Hannah isn't quite fitting in as his replacement. She didn't fit in as Callum's replacement around the house last night either, but I suppose I can't blame her for either.

Mae shakes her head rapidly. "No, no one here will hurt you! Most of them would probably just ignore you. A wolf during the moon isn't much interested in anyone besides their mate, to be honest. But you'd probably get an eyeful."

I raise a brow, but Hannah is the one who says something. "Really? Just out in the open like that?"

Mae shrugs. "Full moon. All decorum kind of goes out the window around here. Like I said, most wolves will ignore everyone who's not their mate. Or an active enemy, I suppose. But the point is, no one is busy perving on anyone else. They're a little focused on their own pleasure."

I flush to hear about it so boldly, but Mae doesn't look embarrassed, so I try not to think about her and Bryce—or anyone else I met here—outside tonight, fucking under the moon. But it's hard. I can see it in her eyes that she's thinking about Bryce. Thinking about what they'll do to each other tonight, and it's made her eyes go soft and hungry.

Well. When she puts it like that, I suppose I will stay inside.

Hannah laughs. "We'll stay in the house then."

Mae grins. "Someday, Marielle, maybe you'll be enjoying it under the full moon, just like the rest of us."

I can't help the image of Callum and I under the moon outside. Maybe up on that clifftop, by the waterfall. No one is around, and he lays me on the grass, the moon caressing our skin as he caresses me and leans in to kiss me, soft and slow and—

Hannah clears her throat, interrupting my thoughts. Good. I don't know where that came from, don't know how I can even think like that right now. "When should we be inside?"

"Sunset," Mae says. "Maybe earlier, just to be safe. Definitely sunset though, if you want to avoid any chance of an eyeful."

"I'll keep that in mind."

I swallow and manage to nod my agreement.

***

I haven't been thinking of Callum like that. I haven't known how to think of Callum—of anyone—like that.

I'd never had the chance to feel those things before the pain and torture of captivity. And now everything I know of sex is rooted in that pain and torture.

I think everyone here knows what happened to me. Maybe Callum told them. Maybe they can sense it. Either way, they're sensible enough to not really bring up the concept of sex, and they never pressure me about being Callum's mate, even if I'm sure they want to say something, telling me to treat him like a mate should.

But when Mae talks about seeing nothing but your mate and being so wrapped up in the passion of connecting under the moonlight, and when Callum talks about him and the wolf both wanting me under the moon, and when everyone says wolves want nothing but to please their mates—

What would being pleased feel like, I wonder?

If it was less humiliating, I could ask Mae. But it is humiliating, especially given that I'm more than three times her chronological age and I have no idea.

Maybe after the moon, I'll be able to work up the courage to ask her.

***

Hannah and I lock ourselves in Callum's house an hour or so before sunset. Neither of us brings up dinner, and I realize with a jolt that today is the first meal I've skipped since I've been here. I wonder if Hannah is skipping for convenience, or if she regularly doesn't eat.

It's strange, not having Callum here to be irrationally pleased whenever I eat something that I discover I like, despite my body not requiring any of the food.

Food feels warm, I think. Warm and secure. Not entirely different to having Callum around has started to feel.

Hannah draws all the curtains, and I frown. I want to see the moon, even if it's just out the window.

Then again, we live in close proximity to three mated pairs. Maybe Hannah has the right idea.

Hannah settles on the sofa, and I look her over. "I didn't realize wolves were so open," she says.

Open. I chuckle. "I'm learning about it too."

"But you're okay with it, right?" she asks, then leans forward slightly. "I know you probably don't feel like you have anywhere else to go, if you weren't. But you could stay with Ryder and I."

It's touching, I think, because they don't know me and Hannah offered this, anyway. But it's unnecessary. "I'm okay with it," I say firmly, with more conviction than I use for just about anything that's not treating patients. "I'm happy here."

Happy might be simplifying things. What do I know about happy?

But I think it might be here. It might be my morning walks with Chase and Mae, and getting to use my skills to treat those in need, and dinners with the family. And it might be sitting with Callum on the couch, barely brushing skin as I read.

And it might be everything else, everything yet to come, everything I haven't thought about yet.

Hannah smiles at me. "I'm glad, then," she says. "I'm glad you found something to make you happy, cousin. But remember you have a place with us if you need it, hm?"

I nod, even as I think that I won't need it.

There's a crashing outside, like bodies falling to the ground, and then a moaning sound so loud that no one can doubt what it might be. Hannah laughs loudly, and I can't help but join in.

"Is that the future you're looking forward to?" she asks, teasing smile in place.

But I can't deny it, blushing, and she just laughs harder.

Chapter Twenty-One

Callum

The cages are like being completely cut off from everything else in the universe.

I already had my hackles up, crossing into a dimension my mate wasn't in. Leaving her at all, considering her state and the upcoming moon, had been hard enough. Entering Demonheim with Chase had been physically painful.

The cages are torture.

There is nothing in the cages. Nothing. I can't smell her, even a small amount lingering on my own skin. I can't see anything, can't hear anything. Even imagining seeing or hearing Marielle falls flat, sensation so dulled in this tortuous space.

It's enough to drive a man mad.

Heath rarely talks about his time here in the cages. But two hundred years ago or so, drunk enough that he didn't remember a word of it the next day, he told me that if you stare into the darkness of the cage long enough, something starts to stare back.

How many nights will I spend here? Ryder will let me out once the moon sets and loosens its hold on me, but I'll be back next month. And the next. And the next.

Because what I said to my brothers remains true. It doesn't matter how awful this place is. I'll bear it forever, if it'll help my mate.

Left with the moon still pulling on my very soul but not even able to properly sustain the thought of my mate as a comfort, I float there, hoping that nothing in the darkness stares back.

***

Ryder releases me in the morning. The warden of the cages, the king of Demonheim, carries a clanking ring of keys on his hip, and they jingle impatiently as he waits for me to right myself and leave the cell.

The door being thrown open changes everything. It's like my soul has come back to me in this space, and I'm able to think and feel again. I take deep, unsteady breaths as I stand upright, making my way shakily to the door.

Ryder raises an eyebrow. "Still think this was a good idea, wolf?"

It takes me a moment to make my voice work. "You telling me you wouldn't do it for your mate?"

He snaps at me half-heartedly, but then leads the way upstairs, out of the cells and into the beautiful palace that covers up the monstrosities hidden below.

"Breakfast?"

"I'm going home." I'm itching to get home. I'm wondering if Ryder would deign to take me, or if it's bad form to call Chase to me so soon after moon-set. But either way, I'm leaving.

Ryder huffs. "And I'm eager to see my mate again, wolf, but hold on. Yours won't be impressed by you at the moment. The cages do a number on you, Callum."

She's seen me covered in blood, I almost argue, but Ryder just gestures to a big gilded mirror hanging above a mantle, and I startle.

I look like I've been locked up for a month. My eyes look a little wild, my hair a tangled mess. Grime has somehow massively accumulated, more than should be possible in a night.

"We'll get you cleaned up and fed, looking like someone your mate won't run from," Ryder says from behind me. "And then you can go tell her about your heroic deed for her."

I bare my teeth at him half-heartedly, because I didn't do this to brag about it after. But he ignores me, even ignores that my fangs are sharper than usual, and just moves over to the table, already laden with food.

***

Fed, cleaned, and dressed properly, Ryder extracts his energy payment from me and takes us back to the village.

I sway on my feet once we land. Perhaps it wasn't a good idea to pay with my own life force after a night in the cages.

Ryder, having no pity for my swaying, steps smartly away from me, turning his attention onto my home, where his mate no doubt still is.

Hannah was here with Marielle last night. I hope it was helpful for her. That meeting her felt valuable to Marielle, or at the very least, they got along.

I force myself to find my footing, then take a deep inhale, scenting my mate inside the house.

Without waiting, I move towards the door, needing to see her, to know she's alright.

Gods above, I'm on edge. Any shit I ever gave to my siblings about their mating bonds, I firmly and completely take back.

The door swings open. Hannah comes out first, running to her mate, and I see him scoop her into his arms from the corner of my eye, but most of my attention is focused on Marielle in the doorway.

She's not dressed for the day yet, wearing a nightgown that comes down to her knees and floats with an eerie, ethereal grace as she descends the front steps and walks towards me.

"You're okay," she murmurs, stopping just in front of me. She looks like she wants to reach for me, but stops herself.

"You're okay too," I say, looking her up and down to check her over, but all that does is reveal that the nightgown top hides nothing from my eyes.

"I'm fine, I—" She shakes her head. "I was worried about you."

I fight to hide my stupid, proud smile. "You were?"

"Of course I was," she says, and there's more complaint in her voice than I've ever heard. She frowns. "I don't like it. You doing that to yourself because of me."

It's a gamble, but I reach out to take her hand, squeezing it lightly. Much to my gratification, she doesn't drop it. "For you. Not because of you."

"What's the difference?"

"Because of puts the blame on you. For you... we haven't even scratched the surface of what I'd do for you yet, Marielle."

Her breath seems to catch, and after a long moment, she swallows. "Come inside," she whispers, and I eagerly, happily, follow my mate into our home.

CHAPTER TWENTY-TWO

MARIELLE

C allum goes absolutely still when I sit so close to him that our thighs brush. I think he stops breathing for a moment, like perhaps I'm a little bird he can startle away by mistake.

"Did something happen, Marielle?" he asks, voice kept deliberately calm and even.

I stop, giving the question its due consideration, even though he has nothing to worry about. He does worry though.

If I was bolder, I'd climb into his lap and make him understand, but I don't know if I can make myself do it, not with any amount of confidence. And he's not going to believe it if I'm not confident.

But climbing into his lap doesn't require words, and I simply don't know what to say. How do I ask for this? How do I tell him I haven't stopped thinking about him since the moment he left, that if he leaves me again I'm going to lose my mind?

"No," I tell him, because at the very least I suppose I can manage to assure him that I'm fine. "It's just..." I shake my head, the words not coming.

"Just what?" he prompts after a moment, voice remaining very level.

Maybe I should climb into his lap and just kiss him. Maybe it would be easier.

"Thank you. For what you did," I start by saying.

"Of course. Anything you need, Marielle."

"I don't want to need that."

"What does that mean, Marielle?" He holds himself still, and says my name like it's a delicate thing. Like it's a delicacy, maybe.

"I want to..." I shake my head. "If I wasn't like this, what would you want from a mating bond?"

"I want whatever you want," he says, and it's so quick, so predictable, that I'm already shaking my head.

"But I think I want it too," I protest. "So what would it look like? To you?"

"If you wanted it?" he checks, and I nod. "If you wanted this..." His eyes slip closed, like he can see it. "I'd probably have already tugged you into my lap. Always want to be closer to you."

I can do that. I maneuver myself into his lap, careful not to poke him with a knee. His eyes open immediately, but his hands come up to gently wrap around me, holding me to him, helping me settle in his lap.

"Marielle..."

"Callum," I say, words barely a whisper. "I think I want to try."

His fingers tighten briefly on my hip. "What does try look like to you, Marielle?"

I shrug. What do I know about successful relationships? All I know is I wanted him here when he was gone. And I like when he smiles.

And I might one day want to feel the moonlight on my skin during the full moon.

"That's why I asked you."

He huffs, and his little laugh breaks the tension a bit. "Well that won't work. We only do this if it's exactly what you want."

"You should want it too," I say, because that is a sticking point.

He just strokes his fingers over my skin through the nightgown. "I was born wanting you," he says. "And am beyond grateful to have you in any way, shape or form now, Marielle. I want it. Believe me."

I want his hands to squeeze me again. I want him to hold me tighter, squeeze me to him.

How else could I respond to that? He's wanted the idea of me since he was born, and even the reality hasn't made him want me less. How else can I respond besides wanting to be squeezed into him as tight as possible?

He doesn't squeeze me. But he does delicately push some of my hair behind my ear, and his fingertips gently stroke over my skin. "Is this okay?" he checks.

"More than okay. Can you... can you..."

"I can do anything you want, Marielle. Ask."

"Kiss me?" I dare to ask it. It hangs between us, a heavy promise.

He doesn't answer, just turns his hand so instead of stroking my face he's cupping it, touching as gently as if my skin was made of gossamer. He leans in slowly, like he's giving me a chance to change my mind.

I don't.

Chapter Twenty-Three

Callum

I f I'm dreaming, no one better ever fucking wake me up.

But I've been in my dreams and I know they're not usually like this. I'm not creative enough to come up with the beautiful, painfully raw determination in Marielle's eyes these last few minutes.

If I was dreaming, this would be perfect. This would never hurt her—I hate that this is painful for her.

She's so fucking brave. It chokes me, rips the air from my lungs, to see her struggling and wanting and choosing this.

I remind myself repeatedly to keep my hands gentle. To not grab her and paw at her, to not squeeze her like I'll never let her go. I manage, because of course I do. Because it's her.

If this was a dream, the kiss would never end. Or it would, but I'd kiss down her neck and to her breasts, and her nightgown would disappear, and I'd keep moving, lower and lower, until she screams my name for the whole town to hear.

Instead, she pulls away and rests her head against the crook of my neck and shoulder, forehead pressed to my skin like she can hide there.

I move my hand from her waist to her back, stroking carefully up and down, feeling her vertebrae through the thin material of that nightgown. "Marielle? You okay?"

It takes her a long moment, but she eventually lifts her head to look at me, and when I see she's smiling, my heart does somersaults. Her smile is thin and tremulous, but it's there.

"Never been kissed before," she says.

Oh. Oh, baby, beautiful, darling—

"How was it?" I ask her, daring, holding my breath, waiting for an answer.

She might have hated it, might be scared by it, might decide she doesn't want it or anything else. And that's okay. Whatever she wants, I remind myself.

"Good," she says, practically a whisper. "It was so good."

Every good moment in my life—every victory, every triumph, every smile and laugh and joy—fades away, pale and obscured by right now.

"Yeah?" I ask, and I'd like to think I keep my voice from sounding desperate. "Do you want to do it again?"

She kisses me in response, leaning back in. Her hands run up my chest, every touch electrifying, even through my shirt. I want her hands on my naked skin; I want to feel her everywhere, be consumed by her—

The kiss is tentative, and I restrain myself from taking control of it. I could make it feel so good; I could make her moan, and I could make her want more than just a kiss. I know I could. But this is her show, her choice, so I restrain myself.

She pulls away but doesn't go far, and her hands move from my chest to my shoulders, around my neck to the back of my skull, playing with the hair there. "Was that alright?" she checks.

There's a grumbling building in my chest, something more akin to purring than I'd ever want to admit. "Alright," I agree, voice almost hoarse, dazed as I watch her lips intently. They curve back into a small smile at my response, and the wolf in me wants to howl his triumph.

"Tell me what this is, Marielle," I beg. "Tell me what you want."

"I don't know," she whispers, but her hand is still in my hair, her body still on my lap, so the words don't feel like such a blow. "I have no idea what I want, I have no idea at all, really. How could I? I never had the chance." Her fingers stop a moment in my hair, and then start again. "I'd like to find out though."

More beautiful words have probably never been spoken. "I'm at your service," I say, and she smiles, but it sounds too light-hearted for what I mean. "Marielle. Whatever you want—I will happily be a part of it. But only if you set the pace. Only if you're clear with me. I can't..." I shake my head, thinking of a thousand worst-case scenarios, a thousand ways I could fuck this up and hurt her. "I can't do this if you don't tell me exactly what to do." I run my hands up and over her waist, a slow drag, feather-light. "This is your show, Marielle."

She sits there, unmoving, for a long moment, but then nods. "I like kissing," she says, and I see it for what it is. Both a boon to me and the only sure footing she has in this.

"Yeah? I do too."

"Kiss me?" she asks, and I'm more than happy to oblige.

Chapter Twenty-Four

Marielle

I like kissing. Or maybe I just like kissing Callum.

There's really no difference between the two for me, because I'll probably never kiss anyone else. Druids and halflings don't have mates like werewolves do, but I can't ever imagine kissing anyone else. Not with how Callum holds me when he kisses me, not when I see the hunger in his eyes, not when I feel his body push against me, yearning.

Not when it lights some fire inside me, something that starts as a warm summer deep inside my belly when he looks at me that way, touches me in his gentle way. And it only burns brighter when he leans in, when he whispers my name or touches his lips to mine. It makes the fire burn brighter and brighter until it is a knotted ball of flames.

He reminds me again and again that I set the pace, that I control the show, that this is my choice, and it's my choice or nothing.

It's a level of kindness that's completely unparalleled, although both Callum and Mae have informed me it's both not a kindness and simply something I should expect from everyone.

But Callum gave it to me, and his kisses make my whole body feel warm. Sometimes warm like a dripping, soft-flowing pool. Sometimes warm like fire in my veins, burning me up.

I think Callum can tell when I get like that. He's a wolf; he can probably smell it. But he's never pushed for more.

I think I want more. I think I want whatever comes next for us, but I don't know how to ask for it. And as much as I want it, it's also a little intimidating.

I think it when he kisses me good morning, soft and slow. Or when he laughs and kisses me after I manage to put one of his soldiers on the ground during a training exercise. Or when he holds me in the evening, stroking my arm as I lean in closer, chasing another kiss. I think about it constantly. I just don't know how to say it.

Callum won't hurt me and I know it. But my body knows to fear pain.

***

Mae has a collection of new clothes spread on the table before her, but she assures me she's well past the point of the enchantment that takes any amount of concentration, and that enchanting her clothes to be warmer doesn't take her much effort these days anyway, so of course we can talk.

Witch magic is just weird. I can feel the hum of her enchantment, but it's distant, almost like someone speaking a foreign language.

"So, what's eating you?" she says, then looks me over long and hard. "Wait. Don't tell me. Mate troubles."

I can feel myself blush at that. "Not troubles, not really," I say, because I don't want to give her the wrong impression. It's not a trouble, or a problem.

She raises an eyebrow. "Then what would you call it?"

"I just don't know what I'm doing," I admit.

She snorts. "Look, I'm not a wolf, but I am mated to one, and I'm surrounded by them, and from what I understand, you could do pretty much anything and Callum would be more than down for it. Unless..." She trails off. "It's not him, it's you, huh? You're not sure what to do for you."

I nod. "I just... I've never done this before, and I want to, but it's a lot. And Callum's so worried about hurting me or scaring me and I—"

"Does he scare you?" She interrupts. "Because I promise you, I know plenty of spells and I can—"

"No!" I interrupt, horrified she could think that. "He never does, he's kind and patient and he's—he's so good, Mae. I just..." I shake my head. "It's a lot."

"You tell him that?" She asks, calmer now, returning to her usual self, all intensity gone.

"He knows," I say. "It doesn't make it any less. And he's not less worried for me."

She looks at me for a long moment, then shrugs. "Look, my best advice? Just sit him down, tell him you want to mess around, and go exactly as far as you're comfortable with. He's a wolf, he'll be happy as hell if you push him exactly where you want him. Trust me. Try it."

I think about it and have to concede it's good advice. "Just like that?"

She nods, turning back to check her enchantment. "Just like that, Marielle. You never know what will happen if you don't take the risk."

The risk. It is a risk. It feels like a risk, but perhaps—not a huge one. Not a dangerous one, like something I can't recover from. Because I know Callum. And I've come to trust Callum.

And I know what I want tonight.

Chapter Twenty-Five

Marielle

Callum is out when I get home.

He's likely with his sister, dealing with some sort of official business, and I don't want to interrupt. That would be silly, and really unnecessary. I can wait.

Of course, despite Mae's best efforts, all waiting does is give me time to build that nervous energy right back up. I practically vibrate right off the couch before I move on to pacing the open room.

Finally, I hear the door open, and I freeze in place for half a second before making my way over there as quickly as I can without running.

"Marielle?" Callum asks, surprise coloring his voice. "What is it?"

I don't answer. I just throw my arms around his neck and pull him down for a kiss.

Not a kiss of greeting. Not something soft and delicate to welcome him home. Instead, something that I'm hoping tells him I want him, that I want to continue this, that I want to take this to bed.

His hands find my waist, pulling me into him, and I lean into it, going up on my toes to push myself as close as I can.

Maybe Mae was right, maybe this can be easy—

"Marielle?" he asks, voice rough as he pulls back.

I chase his lips, but he just kisses my cheek, then rests our foreheads together.

"I want—I want—" I try, and fail.

"What do you want, beautiful girl?"

I bite my lip. "I want you to touch me," I blurt out before I can stop myself. "And to touch you."

Callum goes still. "Are you asking for sex?"

"I—yes? If you want that?"

His smile is slow and dangerous and makes something deep inside me tingle a bit. "You have no idea how badly, Marielle." His hands on my waist squeeze slightly, and his expression gets serious. "But there are rules."

I swallow. "Rules?"

He nods, and one hand slips up my back, stroking gently. "Rules. Like you keep telling me how you're feeling the whole time. You don't lie to me or hide anything. You tell me to stop or change or wait or try something." He kisses my temple, then my cheek, then the corner of my mouth. "You help me make sure I treat you right. Fair?"

I swallow. "Fair."

The grin from earlier, the wicked one that makes my stomach tingle, returns. "Good then," he says, and moves his hands to my hips so he can pick me up without another word.

I squeak, but he pulls me into another kiss, and it's really so much easier when my legs are around his hips and our faces are level. He nips at my lower lip and I part my lips for him, using one hand to brace myself on his shoulder and the other to guide him by his hair.

I expect him to walk me to the bedroom, but we only make it as far as the couch before he deposits me on the edge of the cushion.

Then, keeping smoldering eye contact the whole time, he slides to his knees between my spread thighs.

Chapter Twenty-Six

Callum

I have only one job tonight, and it's a most sacred and honored duty that I have longed for my whole life.

I am going to make my mate come. As many times as she'll let me, however far she'll let me go. I'm going to make her feel so good, be so reassuring, focus on her absolute joy. And when it's over, she'll know that agreeing to be my mate was the right decision.

Like I said, a sacred and most honored duty. The pinnacle of my entire existence, really.

I look up at her with a smile I know is a little wicked.

Her eyes are wide as she looks back down at me, the green seeming brighter than normal as she takes me in. I wonder what it'll take to make her eyes go heavy-lidded with lust, with contentment. I aim to find out.

I place my hands on her knees, itching to push up further but restraining myself. "Can I take your clothes off, beautiful?"

She bites her lip. "Will you take off yours?"

I'm already hard enough to make my jeans uncomfortable just by thinking of touching her, so the answer is obviously yes. I remove my shirt in an instant, looking up at her to gauge her reaction before I begin the rather more awkward process of removing my pants.

Her eyes are still wide as she looks at me, but she doesn't seem scared, or like she's changed her mind. She watched with a steady gaze, and I can't help but nuzzle my face against her knee while I unzip my jeans.

Then I'm struck with whether or not the right choice is to leave my underwear on. But it feels dishonest. I want her underwear off, if she'll let me. I want it desperately, achingly. So I should meet her in turn.

Besides, I have nothing to hide from her. It's all hers, and she should know it.

She stares at me, and I take half a second to wonder if she's ever even seen a naked man before. If they continuously blinded her...

Is it better or worse that she didn't have to watch?

I push the thought away. I won't be angry tonight. Not here, not with her. She doesn't need that from me, and my mate will get exactly what she needs.

"Good?" I check, watching her watch me.

She swallows visibly, nodding slowly. "Yes."

I slide my hands up her calves, to her knees, and watch her shiver. "Good, like I can remove your clothes?"

She nods again, so I push up on my knees, taking the hem of her shirt and pushing it upward. I fight against burying my face into each inch of skin revealed, to smell and kiss and lick, to feel the softness against my face. Next time. Today, I need to see her, all of her.

Each inch of creamy skin calls for me, but I keep a steady pace, pushing her shirt up until her breasts are revealed, then until she lifts her arms so I can remove it entirely. I throw the shirt to the side, not caring where it lands at all, attention entirely focused on what she's now showing me.

Gods. Some of those nightgowns we bought for her don't hide much, but they evidently hid more than I thought. I scrabble at the clasp for her bra, wanting it gone, wanting to see those perfect tits, wanting to hold them, kiss them.

The bra falls away, and she shrugs it off and tosses it aside. I barely notice, my attention captivated by her heavy tits. They heave slightly, her breath coming fast, although from the scent of it, I think it's more arousal than it is nerves.

The wolf in me preens at that, wants to make the smell fill our whole home, every single inch of it covered in her scent.

I run the backs of my fingertips over one nipple, watching her unconsciously push into my touch.

"Good?" I ask again.

She doesn't answer, just nods, and I frown.

"You can touch me however you want," I tell her, taking one of her hands that rests on the couch to prove my point, and guiding it to my head. "Push me, pull me where you want me. Touch me however works for you."

"I... okay. I..." Her hand hesitantly pushes on my head, pushing me closer to her. The touch is soft, easily refused, but I'll never refuse her.

I take my direction well, leaning in to put my mouth on her nipple, sucking gently as my hands find her waist, stroking my fingers across the soft skin there.

I pull away from her nipple, scraping my teeth lightly across it as I go, earning a moan from her that would be enough to get me off for years to come. But if I'm lucky, I'm about to have much, much more.

I move my hands on her waist to her leggings. "These?"

She raises her hips by way of answer, bold enough to take action and I'm so damn proud of her for it, for her chasing what she wants, demanding it. If I am a very, very lucky man, she'll only become more demanding with time.

I help roll down her leggings, catching her panties with them so they both come off together. She kicks them away, leaving herself bare for me.

I drink in the sight. Her cunt is open and wet and glistening for me. The red curls covering her mound are darker than the ones on her head, and her smell is so sweet I want to drown in it.

She squirms under my gaze, and I can't stand the idea of knowing she's uncomfortable. So I take her legs, draw them over my shoulders, and lean in to do what I've been waiting for my whole damn life: feast.

I groan when her taste hits my tongue, sinking further in, using my hands to hold her thighs apart to better serve my aims. I want to taste every inch of her, want to bury myself as deep as I can in her cunt.

She whimpers, and I reward her response by flicking my tongue against her clit, over and over until she bucks against my face. I suck her clit between my lips and manage to get a gasp out of her.

Her taste is worth every moment of longing in my life. It surpasses any dream I've ever had, and I think I could drown in her a happy man.

Regretfully, I pull away. Not far. Just a few inches, just enough that my voice won't be entirely lost in her folds. Her juices coat my lips and chin, and I grin at her. "Keep making noises," I tell her, and even I can hear that my voice is lower. Grumbly, she called it. "Better yet, talk to me."

Her tits really are heaving now, as she draws deep lungfuls. "And say what?" she manages to ask, voice higher and breathier than normal.

"Anything you want. Whatever you like," I tell her. "Tell me what to do, or what you like. Just talk to me."

She bites her lip, but nods, so I dive back in.

Chapter Twenty-Seven

Marielle

He wants me to talk?

I can barely breathe, and he's barely started again. His tongue is teasing me now, avoiding the spot that just made me see stars. Like he's trying to make me react, like he's trying to...

Push me, pull me wherever you want me, he'd said, and, in a complete abandon of any sort of control, I grab his hair and tug him up, up, trying to find that magical spot from before.

"Please," I whimper, and he immediately finds the spot again, flicking it with his tongue once before sucking at it, making my thighs contract around his head.

I'm about to apologize when he groans against me, sending off a fresh wave of this rising feeling in me, this heat coiling tighter and tighter, making my body move, chasing being closer to him. My fingers contract in his hair without me even telling them to, and he groans again.

He likes this. Likes being on his knees, face buried between my legs. Likes me touching him like this.

And gods, but do I like it too.

I knew it would be good. I knew he'd make it good for me, because Callum is a good man, because he wants to give me good things. But I thought...

I don't know what I thought. I didn't think it would be like this. That I would feel like this, want like this. That it would be this physical, this consuming.

The spinning coil of heat in my belly contracts to a single point, suddenly the only point in my whole body I can feel. Then, it's like it explodes outward, all my muscles suddenly alive again, the sensation dragging through me.

"Callum," I gasp, and I know my thighs are squeezing him, but I can't help myself, bucking against his face as he continues to lick me, tongue dipping lower.

After a long, long moment, I release my grip on him, then push him gently back by the hair. He grins up at me, his face obscenely wet. His eyes are bright with happiness.

"Marielle, you taste delicious," he purrs, and he leans forward again, as if unconsciously, before he shakes himself. "Was that good, beautiful girl?"

It takes a moment to find the ability to speak. "I never knew it could feel like that," I manage.

Something dark crosses his eyes, there and gone. "It should always feel that good," he says, then considers. "Maybe even better. Only our first time, after all. I'm bound to get better with practice."

I want to laugh at the idea that he could be any better, but oh gods, the thoughts he plants in my mind. I'd be unconscious if he was any better. I'd simply pass out.

I shift slightly, feeling the wetness between my thighs, the slight swelling of my sex. My movement is slight, but it must be a magnet for Callum, because his eyes snap right back to me.

"I'm a mess now," I say, as if that's an explanation.

His eyes go heavy, and I can't help but stare. "I'd offer to clean you with my tongue," he says, voice husky. "But that might be counterproductive."

It would be. But oh, I can't help but squirm again at the thought.

He sees it and smiles slowly, wickedly. "Can I taste you again, then, Marielle? No sense cleaning up if I'm just going to get you all messy again."

I swallow, trying to keep my wits about me, trying to keep my thoughts in order. "What about you?" I ask.

"What about me?" He returns, running his nose along my thigh.

"Don't you want..." I trail off, not sure what to say.

He stops, presses a kiss just above my knee, and then looks up at me. "I'm the happiest I've ever been, Marielle. Right here, right now."

I shake my head. "You didn't get anything out of that."

"Didn't get anything?" He asks incredulously. "Marielle, I've dreamed of doing that. And right now, looking at your pretty little cunt, smelling it, tasting it on my tongue, I can't think of a single other thing I want to do for the rest of my life."

"Oh." I manage to shake myself out of that declaration, as oddly compelling as it might be. "But I want..."

"What do you want, beautiful?" he prompts me when I can't finish. "Because whatever it is, it's yours. I promise."

He means it, too. He means it in every single interaction we've had since the day we met. Callum is honest like that.

"Come up here?" I ask, and he's scrambling up before I'm even done asking, sitting next to me on the couch. He seems to hesitate for a minute, probably trying to determine how much space to leave between us.

I settle it by pulling him closer until our naked thighs and hips brush. He hisses at the contact—interesting, considering how close he was to me just a moment ago—but then leans into it.

He pulls me into his lap when we kiss, holds me whenever he thinks he can get away with it. And even before the kissing started, I'd have to be blind not to notice how much he liked being near me, how he'd freeze and then melt when my foot brushed his leg or our fingers touched.

Good. I like that he reacts like that, that I can see and feel how he wants to be close to me.

I look him over. He's a mess, hair wild from my fingers and face messy. His chest is still moving from rapid breaths, and I let my gaze dip lower.

Hard. He's so hard, dear gods, he's so hard it must hurt him.

I want to ask him, but instead I reach out hesitantly, and his entire body freezes. I think he stops breathing.

At my first tentative touch, his hips jerk towards my hand and he lets out a sound that he tries to squash behind his lips. He's only partially successful.

I move my fingers just slightly, a delicate touch, and he moves his hips again. "Harder," he says between gritted teeth. "You can touch it harder, Marielle. More. Please."

So I wrap my hand all the way around him, and hesitantly begin to stroke.

He feels good in my hand, the skin soft even as he's hard. He can't seem to stop moving his hips, little aborted rolling motions that make me unwittingly think about what he'd be like inside of me.

Would it be good? If he was rolling his hips like that against me, moving inside me, would I like it? Would it feel good?

I didn't really think any touch could truly feel good. I didn't expect the physical sensations of today. I expected to feel closer to him, like maybe I was cementing the bond with my mate. But I never thought my body would feel this good, this alive.

He groans again, and I press my thighs together as I keep stroking him.

"That's it, beautiful," he says, voice low and grumbly. "Just like that, oh, I never thought it'd be this fucking good..."

I look away from my hand on him to his face, watching him look at me, eyes firmly fixated on my hand.

Then, like he can feel my stare, his eyes snap to mine, and they're full of something dark and wild and incredibly tempting. "Perfect mate," he rasps. "Beautiful, perfect mate, I'm—"

His words stop and an actual growl works its way out of him, his hips pushing towards my hand before he twitches in my grasp and comes all over my hand.

I stroke him through it, tentatively, but he doesn't stop me until a long moment later, one of his hands gently taking my wrist and pulling me away. His eyes focus on my hand for a long moment, then he looks up at me.

"How was that?" he asks, and he has a half smile on his face, but I can hear his sincerity in the question.

I don't know how to tell him, how to explain it to him, how to talk about how I didn't know my body would feel like this, could feel like this. So instead I lean in and kiss him, once, twice, a third time, this time long and hard and deep, hopefully telling him everything I wish I could just say.

"It was perfect," I tell him, and then I kiss him again.

CHAPTER TWENTY-EIGHT

CALLUM

I don't want to get out of bed, but the knock at our door is persistent.

And it still takes nearly fifteen long minutes of knocking to convince me to go down. What can I say? There's a lot of compelling reasons to stay in bed, too.

Mostly it's my warm mate in my arms, her red hair loose for sleeping and all over the pillows and pressed against my face, tickling my nose but smelling so sweet. She's warm and soft and actually clutches at the arm I have around her, like she somehow has to convince me not to let go.

After first sharing a bed with her, I was surprised by what she could sleep through. I'd thought someone who went through what she did would have vigilance beaten into her bones.

But she sleeps through everything, including me moving in the night or my phone ringing. She sleeps through her own nightmares.

I'd wanted to go kill something when I'd brought it up and she'd told me, very quietly, that some things are simply easier to sleep through when you can't stop them anyway.

So the knocking hasn't woken her, but it's annoying the hell out of me.

The sooner I make them go away, the sooner I can get back to holding Marielle. Maybe I can even convince her to start the day off in a more exciting way, like with my head between her thighs.

That's what I'd been dreaming of when the knocking first woke me, after all.

Grumbling, I carefully take my arm back from her grip, giving her my pillow to hold in the meantime. She clutches it greedily.

I find pants, a tall order given that neither of us had paid much attention to where they'd gone the night before, and pull them on before going to check the door.

It's Bryce, looking even more grumpy than normal. "Getting your dick wet isn't an excuse to leave me out here this long."

A growl rips through me, low and vicious. Not a threat, not really—at least not a mortal one, which is usually the only kind a wolf would bother to make. But I suppose there's always an exception for siblings.

"You of all people should know full well not to intrude on the newly mated," I snarl.

He looks me up and down, slow, but at least has the manners to not say what he can undoubtedly see and smell; that as much progress as Marielle and I have made, as happy as we truly, genuinely are, these past two weeks haven't seen us fully mated yet.

Marielle, it turns out, likes sex. She's liked everything we've done, but we're still taking this slowly, and I'm reluctant to take any steps that could cause her even the slightest pain.

She seemed so surprised that she could even enjoy herself, and I'm hesitant to push for more. We take this at her pace.

"I'm doing you a favor, asshole, remember?" he snaps, but it's more out of obligation than anything else. He shoves a box into my hands. "Since you can't be bothered to leave your damn bed to pick it up yourself."

Leave my bed. Right. Like any newly mated wolf is going to walk away from his mate so soon. Bad enough that I'll have to leave her for the full moon in just three more days.

I look down at the box, the dark-stained wood carefully inlaid with her name at the top, and nod.

Most mates get jewelry, and I have plans to buy her the jewels she deserves. But for now, I know what she really wants.

I slam the door in my brother's face, not feeling at all bad considering he and Mae practically abandoned us for three years after they first mated, and go back upstairs.

Marielle is awake, green eyes blinking up at me, still hazy with sleep. She props herself up on an elbow. "What're you doing awake, beautiful?" I ask, setting the box down on my bedside table, ready to crawl back into bed with her.

She shrugs. "You left."

And that does something to my heart. That I help her sleep well, that I am enough to wake her.

I pull her back into my arms. "Want to sleep some more?"

She pushes back against me, and the very deliberate wiggling of her ass is a clear enough answer. "Not really."

"No? What do you want then? Breakfast?" She's still not good at saying it, as much as she's been enjoying everything we do together. The way she flushes is adorable.

But also, I want her to say it. Every time, I want her to tell me.

And she's so damn brave, because she does. "You," she says, not turning to look at me, leaving me to picture the blush on her face. "I want you."

So damn brave. "Yeah?" I ask as gently as I can, nuzzling the pointed tip of her ear as I speak. "How do you want me?"

This is where it'll get trickier. She'll tell me to decide, try to pawn it off, and I'll have to push back and—

"Would you..." She squirms, but this is definitely not the deliberately seductive move from a moment ago. "Would you lick me?"

A fucking dream come true. "It would be my absolute pleasure," I tell her.

"And maybe your fingers too?"

I'd worked up to putting a finger inside her, when she's already dripping for me and on edge, when I want to drive her just that much higher. She's so small, and has experienced so much pain, come to expect it, that I want to be careful. But I nod against her neck, breathing "yeah" against her skin while I press kisses there.

I debate for a moment how I want to please her this morning, kissing and sucking at her neck while I think. I want to roll over onto my back and pull her up to straddle my face, continuing the delicious dream Bryce's rude knocking had interrupted. But it's not the best angle to really get her off with my fingers, and she'd explicitly asked for that. No way am I going to deny her what she'd asked for. Not in any world, but especially not when it takes her such courage.

So I roll her onto her back, sliding my pillow under her back, and remove the shirt she slipped on last night. My shirt, actually, positively dwarfing her. I fucking love seeing her in it.

Wolves are possessive, but this close to the full moon? I can barely think of anything else.

I tug the shirt off her, revealing her glorious tits. I palm each one, squeezing lightly, making her breath hitch before I trail my fingers down her stomach, slow and seductive and waiting for that breath hitch again. There. That's it.

I skim past where she really wants me, where I want desperately to be, and curl my hand around her soft thigh. Her thighs are like heaven, all soft and pillow-like, and I could touch just them for hours. But for now, I guide her leg over my shoulder, opening her up for my greedy eyes. And hands. And mouth.

"That's it," I murmur, attention fully drawn to her cunt, already wet for me. "So beautiful and open for me, just waiting for me to make you feel good, hm? Such a perfect mate."

She moans again, and it's absolutely fucking beautiful, music to my ears. I could stare at her all day, but before she starts squirming, before she gets truly uncomfortable, I lean in to lick along her cunt, one teasing lick. My eyes flick up her body, where her head's already thrown back, her hands fisting the sheets, and then I set in with purpose, until all I can taste is her.

When she's truly wet enough to soak my face, when she's lost in the haze of pleasure, I slide one finger into her, relishing as she grinds down to meet it, using my face and my hands for her pleasure, as she always should.

Her hand leaves the sheets and grasps at my hair. She's not really tugging, more like clenching, then releasing, then clenching again, and I hum against her in response. She bucks against my face.

"Oh, I—more," she moans, her hips rocking again. "More, please, Callum, more!"

Like I'll ever be able to refuse that. I'm a thousand years old, and I could live another thousand, two, three, with her by my side, in our bed, and still not be able to refuse that.

So I slide in another finger, teasing her with it for a long moment before slowly slipping it inside her tight, warm heat, and I can't stop myself from moaning against her clit as I feel her muscles clench around me.

What will that feel like around my cock? Already I think I could come, just from the way she squeezes my fingers.

Everything about her is so fucking perfect.

I've only ever slipped a finger into her when she was already about to come. But now I'm two fingers deep and she wants it, wants more, is rocking her hips, feeling them stretch her inside, and I crook them, searching for that spot inside of her.

"Callum Callum Callumcallumcallum..." She practically chants my name, and I know then that I've found it.

I feel her thigh tense up over my shoulder first, and then her inner muscles clamp down on my fingers. Her hands squeeze my hair, and her hips buck errati-cally against me, chasing that high while she pants my name, and I lap in eager bliss as she comes all over my fingers and face.

After a long, long moment, I reluctantly pull away, slowly removing my fingers and bringing them to my mouth to lick clean, watching her the whole time. Her face and chest are red, almost as red as her hair, and her mouth is hanging ever so slightly open, taking in lungfuls of air. A stupid sense of male pride fills me, and I know that if I accomplish nothing else for the rest of my long life, I'll still always have this moment.

"I'd be down for starting every single morning like this," I say, my voice rough and low.

I push myself up her body, carefully removing her leg from my shoulder, hovering over her. She smiles shyly up at me.

"Only if I can return the favor," she murmurs.

My breath catches. My shy, beautiful, brave mate.

116

I swallow. "What'd you have in mind?"

Chapter Twenty-Nine

Marielle

In the end, I wasn't brave enough to say what I wanted. I wanted to ask to put him in my mouth, but I couldn't make myself.

From what I understand, men like that, but what if I'm not good at it? Sex is a skill like anything else, and I certainly don't have any practice at it. Not at making it enjoyable for anyone, at any rate.

Even so, when he comes on my hand, hips rocking and face slack with pleasure, I don't feel the disappointment in myself I've felt so often. I didn't fail. I just haven't succeeded yet.

And I already know that I'll have many more chances.

He holds me to him in the afterglow, stroking his large hands over the skin of my arm, moving from shoulder to the delicate crease of my inner elbow, and back again, a slow, rhythmic motion lulling me almost back to sleep.

"What's in the box?" I ask, catching sight of it on the nightstand, remembering at last that something had prompted him to leave the bed this morning.

To my disappointment, he sits up instead of just answering, leaving me feeling cold and bereft. "It's a gift."

"A gift?" What more could he possibly give me?

He shrugs. "I thought you'd like this. I ordered it a while ago, but these things take time. And Bryce picked it up for me." He picks up the wooden box and turns to me, offering it. "Here. Open your present."

I sit up so I can take it, running my fingers along the fine wood. "What is—"

He laughs, cutting me off. "Open it and find out, beautiful!"

So I do, carefully prying open the lid.

Inside sit two finely crafted daggers, the metal polished to a gleam, the edges wickedly sharp. They are clearly incredibly finely made, and I can tell without even lifting them that the balance will be perfect.

"They're beautiful," I whisper, lifting one just to confirm it's as perfect as it looks. It might somehow be even better.

"You clearly enjoy them," he says, as if he's trying to downplay his gift. "And you should have your own. Good ones, not whatever is lying around. Your own."

I carefully place the dagger back in the box before throwing my arms around him. He freezes for a long moment and then hugs me back. "Callum, they're the most beautiful things I've ever seen," I say. "Thank you."

He clears his throat. "Anything for you," he says. "Do you want to try them out?"

I really, really do. But there's one thing I want more, and I turn his head so I can kiss him.

It's nearly an hour before we dress to go outside.

***

I haven't tested myself against Callum yet. Callum has watched me against Bryce, against Jake and Honor and a few other soldiers, but he's never stepped up to fight me himself.

Callum is fast. I understand now what the others have told me, the things I haven't fully grasped even after watching him on the training grounds. Celia sits on the metaphorical throne. Bryce, grumpy and standoffish as he can be, is their emissary and diplomat. Heath handles the things no one else would want to. And Callum...

Callum is an army unto himself. I know all wolves are warriors, that most every wolf trains from childhood, but Callum is something else. The man is faster, stronger, and more predatory than any of the wolves I've ever seen.

Callum doesn't go easy on me. Well, technically speaking, he probably does, because teeth and claws don't join this fight, and I have a feeling that, if he really wanted to, he could have me on the ground in seconds. He has a thousand years or so of practice, after all.

But even knowing that, his hits are hard, his moves clever, and I feel actually tested, pushed, and challenged as I try to move around him.

Dodging and deflecting blows is making me work up a sweat, and I can barely keep up the energy to strike back—strikes that he deftly avoids every single time.

I try to trip him as I move to dodge a blow, and he easily side-steps, but looks impressed.

"You fight dirty." It sounds like a compliment when he says it.

I don't respond, but to prove it, I try to kick dirt into his face.

It doesn't stop him; instead, he drops his blade, catches my foot, and pushes me to the ground.

I land with an oof, but I know if Callum really wanted to do damage, he could have easily broken my leg. "Not bad," he says, and I'm gratified to see some sweat on his brow.

I swipe at his knees, and, not expecting it, he goes down on top of me.

"Gods!" He falls, rapidly trying to control his descent so he doesn't land on me. He manages it, falling right beside me, and then he reaches over and grabs me, hauling me on top of him.

I place my hands on his chest, using them to push me up enough to look into his eyes. "Thank you for the present," I murmur, kissing him softly.

His eyes go soft and unfocused. "If you look at me like that, I'm getting you presents every damn day."

I laugh. "That might be a bit much."

He growls and rocks his body, rolling so I'm on my back again and he's hovering over me, bracing himself on his elbows.

"I think," he says, leaning down to run his nose along my neck, "that that sounds like the perfect amount of presents."

I reach up and run a hand through his hair, scratching my nails along his scalp. "Do you think I won't look at you like this without gifts?"

Because I will. Gods, I feel like I'm always looking at him now. As Mae teases, with hearts in my eyes.

Druids and halflings don't have mates, but I think I've found mine, anyway.

I know it's fast. I know that I came from a terrible situation, and then immediately fell for the first person to show me any kindness in two hundred years. I know all of it.

I still fell for him. Hard and fast and all-consuming. And really, with the way he looks right back at me, I know it's mutual.

Case in point, he pulls back from my neck, pushing into my hand still in his hair, just to stare at me. His eyes are soft and I could stare into them all day.

"I'll do anything you want for you to look at me like that," he says, voice husky, and the scary thing to me is, I think he means it. Anything. Wolves are intense.

Anything. He's said things like this before, but I suddenly realize that he means anything I ask. Callum, prince of werewolves, thousand year old warrior, would do anything I asked of him.

Anything. I promise myself right there that I won't ever abuse it.

I move my hand so I'm cupping his jaw, running my thumb over his face in a way that has his eyes drooping closed and his face tilting into my hand. "Kiss me?" I ask.

He falls on me like a starving man. His kiss makes me lose focus of everything but him, and my hand makes it back into his hair, holding him exactly where I want him.

He finally pulls away, but I don't let him go far. Instead, he kisses my jaw, then sucks at my ear. "Gods, I'm going to miss you," he mutters.

That stops my thoughts cold. I'd just been about to ask him to take me back inside, or abandoning all sense of decorum and rutting against him right here on the grass. But miss me? Where would he possibly be going?

"What?"

He pulls back, and I reluctantly release my hold on his hair so he can move. "Full moon is coming," he says, voice gentle.

Something inside me stings at that. I had just assumed...

Well. Even I know what they say about assuming.

"I thought we'd..." I don't know how to explain it. I still can't talk about it, even as much as I want it. And it's worse right this moment, because he's going to go back to Demonheim, instead of making love to me on the full moon.

"Marielle, I'd like nothing in the world more than that," he assures me, and he leans back down to press a kiss to the corner of my mouth.

"You can have it, then."

"No, I can't," he says, pulling back, seemingly reluctantly. "The full moon won't allow me to be gentle with you, Marielle. And we've never done this before and you deserve gentleness. Especially for the first time. Until you're comfortable."

I want to tell him he can take me to our bed right now. That he can make love to me now, be as gentle as he wants, and we can talk about the full moon tomorrow.

But is he wrong? Am I ready for that?

I don't know, and I can't say anything.

He kisses the corner of my mouth again. "I'll make you feel so good under the moon, Marielle. Someday. When you're ready. That's a promise."

I swallow at the heat in his words. "But not this time."

"No," he says, and I think that's genuine regret I hear in his voice. "Not this time."

I sigh, but he's right about this. "Alright," I agree, wrapping both arms around his neck, playing with the hair at the nape of his neck. "Next full moon."

"If you're ready," he agrees, already leaning back down to kiss my neck.

He's so good to me. Always thinking of what I need. And maybe he's right that I'm not ready today or tomorrow. And he'd go back to Demonheim next month and the one after and the one after and forever if I needed it, I know without asking.

But I have a good feeling about next month.

CHAPTER THIRTY

CALLUM

C hase gives me a mocking bow, leaving me in Ryder's front parlor. "Magical taxi service, final stop," he says. Then he straightens and looks at me a lot more seriously. "After the moon, you, Marielle, and I need to have a conversation."

The grip of the moon is already starting to latch onto me, but I force myself to focus on Chase. "You found something?"

"Maybe. And you two will need to decide what happens next. But not tonight."

"Not tonight," I agree, and Chase doesn't wait for any more confirmation before disappearing, not even sticking around to greet his king.

We're cutting it a little close to the moon tonight, but I had trouble saying goodbye to Marielle.

If it was nearly impossible last month, this month is a thousand times worse. It's still undoubtedly the right choice for her, but it's still hard.

Ryder appears, a frown on his face. "You're back."

I try to smile and know I fail miserably. "Have an open cell?"

***

It's just as bad this time as it was last time.

I should smell like her. Her scent should permeate every inch of my skin from being so close to her all the time, from making her come on my fingers three times in a row just hours ago. But the moment the cage door closes, all my senses are lost. I can't smell her. I can't sense her at all, and the wolf in me loses control.

I never asked Heath if the wolf ever took control down here, and he's certainly never volunteered the information. And I've never fully ceded control to the wolf, never been in great enough distress for the wolf to feel it necessary, but tonight—

I feel a hair's breadth from it happening.

***

When Ryder releases me in the morning, he makes me eat and change and clean up before he offers to take me anywhere. "You'll scare her," is all he says.

Hannah, who's reading at the table, tuts. "She's made of tougher stuff than that," she disagrees, but pushes a plate of bacon at me anyway.

I eat it. And accept the shower and the change of clothes before bargaining with Ryder for a ride home.

I don't think I'd scare her. But, as much as I want to go back to her immediately, I need to hide the evidence of how hard this is on me.

If she really ends up wanting to participate in the full moon next month, I will consider myself the luckiest wolf in the world. But if she needs more time, then I will ensure she has it exactly as much as she needs, and I won't sway her decision by forcing her to feel bad for me.

***

When I get back, I practically stagger into her arms, which might undercut my decision not to show her how hard this is. But I can hardly care. I bury my face in her neck. There. There's her scent. I want to bathe in it, soak in it, let it fill my pores and my senses, so I'm surrounded by it again.

124

She clings to me tightly, her hands pushing under my borrowed shirt, desperate for skin-on-skin contact. I oblige her, slamming our front door shut and stripping my shirt off, then scooping her up under her thighs, encouraging her to wrap them around my waist as I carry her up the stairs and to bed.

I'm going to make good on my vow to soak in her scent.

Chapter Thirty-One

Marielle

I laugh as he carries me to our bed, holding onto him as he moves, nearly running to get me there. "Missed me?"

"That's putting it mildly," he grunts, pushing up my shirt before laying me down across the bed and watching me hungrily. "Marielle, I want—"

"I want to ask you something," I interrupt before I can change my mind.

He goes still. "Alright then. What is it?"

"Can I—would you want—I want to suck you," I say, almost all in one breath.

He doesn't answer for a moment, and I start to squirm. "I thought you might like that, but if you don't, we don't need to—"

"I want it, Marielle," he interrupts, and his voice is strained. "I just was thinking about getting my mouth on you. Just switching gears."

"Oh."

He grins, then seems to come to a conclusion. "Fuck it. Best of both worlds."

"What's that mean?" I try to ask, but he's already moving, kicking off his clothes. I pull off the rest of my clothes too, watching him.

He lays down next to me, then grabs me to position me so I'm over his face, looking down his body. "You do whatever feels good to you," he says, voice muffled from under me. "And I'm going to soak myself in your pretty little cunt."

I shiver. "I'll hurt you," I protest, thinking of my weight against his face. There's no way I can be careful and make sure I don't crush him, not when I know how good his tongue always makes me feel.

"No, you won't." And to emphasize his point, he grabs my hips and pulls me tighter to his face.

I gasp as his tongue licks over my clit, and it takes me a long moment to get my bearings. Whatever feels good to me, he'd said. And I want to suck him.

I lean forward, doing my best to keep my balance so I don't accidentally hurt him, and hesitantly lick over the tip.

He groans between my legs, and I do it again, then again, before working the tip into my mouth.

I want him to like this. I want to be good at this, because I know I'm currently making a mess all over Callum's face, and I want to give him that. I want to have that. I want to have the ability to make my mate as crazy as he makes me.

So I trace the tip with my tongue again, and then try to take him deeper.

And promptly gag.

His mouth on me stills, and his hands on my hips tug at me gently, as if pulling me away from him. "You okay?" he asks, voice muffled from against my inner thigh.

"I'm fine." I am. I'm fine. Just didn't expect that.

"Go slow, if you're going to continue," he says. "Just focus on the tip. Use your hand." And then, the lesson in fellatio apparently over, he positions me back over his face and dives back into my folds.

Okay. I lean back down and suck the tip again, taking Callum's groan as encouragement. Then I shift my weight to my left hand, freeing my right to wrap around the parts of his shaft I can't reach with my tongue. This part I've done before, dozens of times now, and it takes just a moment to match the movements of my hand to the movements of my tongue, and I'm rewarded with a groan against my clit and tiny movements of Callum's hips that he can't quite suppress.

After a few minutes of this, Callum growls loud enough that the vibrations shake through my whole body. Then he grabs my hips and flips me onto my back on the bed, pushing my knees apart so he can kneel between them.

I look up at him, looming over me, and he takes himself in hand, stroking rapidly. His eyes don't leave mine as he continues to stroke, and then, with a cry of my name, he comes all over my chest.

He looks at me for a second as I look at him. And then, all he says is, "So godsdamned beautiful," before positioning himself so his mouth is on me once more, and I'm shouting his name as he sends me over the edge.

Chapter Thirty-Two

Callum

Hours later, I certainly can smell her everywhere on me again. I wrung two orgasms out of her with my tongue, and her wetness is clinging to my lips and chin still, and I debate if it's worth the grief she and everyone else would give me if I didn't clean it up for the rest of the day.

Honestly, the wolves among us might even understand. Oh sure, they'd give me grief because they're my siblings, but what wolf doesn't dream of drowning in their mate's scent?

She smells like me too, again, and I can't tell if I'm prouder of my come still on her glorious tits, or her come on my face.

I reach over to grope her left breast, wanting to worship the soft flesh, wanting to rub my come into her skin and rub her nipple until she moans, and watch the mound bounce as she gasps for breath when I pinch her just right.

She laughs breathlessly. "You're insatiable."

I freeze immediately. "You want me to stop?"

"I didn't say that. But are we going to stay here all day?"

Fuck yes we are. If I have my way, if the universe gave me everything I wanted, we'd get weeks of just this.

But I sigh, and give her breast a sorrowful pat, a promise to return to business later. "Chase wanted to see us today," I say, looking at the clock on the nightstand. "Think they're awake?"

Lucky bastards, worn out and recovering from the full moon.

I remind myself that I'm waiting for Marielle, and that I'll do anything for her. And also, whenever she gives me the gift of being inside her under the full moon, I'll tire her out so much that there's absolutely no chance at all anyone would expect her to be up and moving the next day.

Marielle sits up and stretches, a move that thoroughly distracts me from any other thought. "Guess we'll find out," she says, moving towards the bathroom while I lie in bed, watching her hips move. "Are you coming?"

Not yet, but I guarantee we both will be, would be a cheesy answer, so I keep my mouth shut and follow her.

***

Chase is awake and even dressed. He has a stunning bruise poking out from the collar of his shirt, which he puts no effort into hiding. I'm quietly impressed Heath managed that, given how fast we all tend to heal.

"Was wondering when you'd come looking for me," he says, letting us into their house. It's similar enough to ours in layout, and he points us to an old leather couch.

Marielle sits so she's pressed against me, knee to shoulder, and holds my hand in hers, and I think I might burst right out of my skin.

Chase notices, because of course he does. "Cute," is all he says, before sitting in the armchair across from the couch. "Alright, so, I found something."

"Something about...?" Marielle asks.

He sighs. "You, Marielle. I've had a lead for a few weeks, but now I know it's true. First, I found your father."

Marielle squeezes my hand tight enough to almost be painful. "Where is he?" she asks, taking the words right out of my mouth. Except she sounds nervous, and I just feel fury.

130

I don't want to leave her so soon after getting back, but I'll absolutely go kill him tonight. It won't take too long; I'm sure every family member would be more than glad to help.

"Dead, Marielle. I can tell you where he's buried, even."

That takes some of the wind right out of my sails, and I turn to focus on Marielle, who's frozen at the news.

"Dead?" she asks after a long moment. "You're sure?"

Chase nods. "Dead sure, I promise. Dead as a doornail, in the ground. I don't know the details, but I don't think he lasted long after what he did to you."

That's some justice, I suppose.

Marielle nods tremulously. "Thank you for telling me. Is it wrong that that's comforting?"

"No," Chase and I both say at the same time.

Chase gives her a moment to collect herself, then says, "Marielle, there's more. I found Theo."

There's a sharp intake of breath from her, and the hand around mine squeezes tight enough that her knuckles go white. "Did you find where he's buried?" she asks, and she's trying so hard to keep her voice steady.

Before I found her, she had one person in two hundred years that she gave a damn about. One person who'd treated her even remotely right. And it's not fair that she has to do this, even if she already knew he was dead.

I want to pummel Chase for bringing it up, as completely unfair as that is, as much as this is my own fault, as much as Heath would kill me for it. But this is making Marielle sad, and it seems my natural response to that is to fight for her. Even when it doesn't make any sense.

"Marielle, he's not dead."

The silence hangs heavily around us. She shakes her head. "He was human," she says, slowly. "Humans—even now they rarely reach a century. Theo was young two centuries ago. He's dead."

"He's not," Chase says, slowly and reassuringly, leaning towards us, hands clasped between his knees. "This is why I waited so long. Why I had to be sure."

I swallow. "What happened to him?"

"You said you helped him escape with a lover, right?" Marielle nods. "Did you ever meet the lover?"

She shakes her head, slowly, and I start seeing the pieces fall together.

"Vampire?"

The one species that can make more of themselves, who propagate not just through birth but also biting.

Chase nods. "Not just any vampire. Marielle, your brother has gone up in the world. He's mated to Silas Emrick." When he sees she has no idea who he is, he explains, in a gentle voice I rarely hear from him, "Think like these guys. Just for vampires."

Vampire royalty. Marielle's brother mated himself to vampire royalty.

There's a scuffing noise, and I look up to see Heath, very much rumpled from last night's activities, leaning against the doorway, arms crossed and eyes narrowed. "We're tangling with the Emricks?"

"Marielle's brother might be one by marriage now," Chase says, not turning.

"Do vampires do marriage?" I ask.

Heath frowns. If anyone here would know anything about species we try not to interact with much, it would be these two. "Oh, they do," he says shortly, not elaborating. He walks closer and lays a hand on Chase's shoulder. "We haven't had much contact with the Emricks for the last few centuries. More a you leave us alone, we'll do the same type of thing."

"Why?" Marielle finally asks, blinking slowly as she seems to come back to focus. "What's wrong with them? Is it..." She hesitates, biting her lip. "Would they hurt Theo?"

"Not if he's Silas' mate," Chase says. "Which he is. That much I know. Marielle, your brother found himself a prince. He's not only safe and alive, he's... well, trust me. The vampires know luxury."

An understatement.

Heath frowns. "Did you make contact with him, Chase?"

"Not yet. That's up to Marielle."

She takes a deep, shaky breath, squeezing my hand tighter. "Did you see him?"

Chase nods, a small dip of his head. "I did. Briefly. Best not to linger around vampires uninvited for too long."

"Does he look okay?"

"He looks good, Marielle. He's a vampire, and he's a prince-consort. Trust me, he's well fed and well taken care of."

Marielle squeezes her eyes shut and goes absolutely silent. It goes on so long I almost shoo Heath and Chase out of their own living room so I can get her space, but she finally speaks up. "I'll leave him alone then."

Chase opens his mouth, but I quell him with a look. He snaps it shut and nods once slowly, conceding to me.

"Is that it?" Marielle asks.

"All I have right now," Chase confirms. "If you want me to find out more about him, it wouldn't be impossible."

It would be difficult, though. Vampires aren't known for letting others poke into their affairs.

Marielle doesn't take him up on it. She just nods, says "thank you" in a quiet voice, and gets up to leave.

I follow her, as I always will, and ignore the worried looks from my family.

CHAPTER THIRTY-THREE

MARIELLE

Theo is alive. Theo is alive and mated to a prince. Theo is a vampire.

Theo never came back for me. But I never should have expected him to.

We weren't equals in that house. We may have both been under my father's thumb, but Theo was a human whose life was continuously in danger. And I was just me. I had power, of a sort. I wasn't like him. Of course he never came back for me. Even if he was apparently in a position where it would have been possible.

"Are you angry at him?" Callum asks me once we're back home. He's moving around the kitchen, and I'm sitting at the counter, watching. He's always cooking for us, always making sure there's food, and I've long since given up protesting that I don't need it. Not when he looks at me so softly when I accept it from him.

Maybe I should learn to cook. It never felt like a practical skill before.

"At who?"

"Theo." Callum doesn't beat around the bush. It's not in his nature.

"I'm conflicted," I settle on.

He sets down the knife he was using to dice potatoes and turns fully to me. "Explain it then."

I have his full, undivided attention, and I really feel like this might be as important to him as it is to me. Like it matters, for real, and not just in my mind.

"I had no right to expect anything else," I tell him, trusting him with my honesty. "He took care of himself. That's all I should expect. And I'm happy that he's alive. Okay. Happy, hopefully."

I wonder if his mate is as good as mine. Callum, Heath, and Chase seemed a little reserved about vampires, but that doesn't mean that Theo isn't happy. Is he? He ran away with Silas when he was desperate. Would he still choose him today?

If his mate is half as good as Callum is, who has abandoned his cooking to come sit next to me, then Theo is surely happy indeed.

That warms me a bit, to think that, whatever else, his life worked out for the better. But that warmth might also be Callum's big hand on my thigh.

"But?"

I shrug. "I was stuck there too." Not in the same way. I was the halfling child, the bargaining chip. Theo was the human slave. No one would ever argue that it was his job to save me, least of all me.

But I was trapped there too. And it turned out so badly for me.

Before I know what's happening, Callum has pulled me into his lap, a balancing act on the stools at the counter, but I know he won't let me fall. His strong arms hold me tight, and I let myself collapse completely against him.

"So, are you mad at him?" he repeats the question, the heart of the matter.

His breath fans across my neck, and I wonder how anyone could be mad about anything, given that. But I try to focus on the question.

"I don't want to be."

"Fair enough," he says, pressing a kiss against my pulse. I tilt my head to give him more room, but he pulls back a bit. "The beauty of living forever is that you can change your mind later, Marielle. If you want to see him tomorrow, in a year, a century, we'll make it happen."

He's right, and it's reassuring, and something inside me relaxes. No decisions have to be made today.

"Let's find a distraction," he proposes. I nod, expecting his hands to creep up under my shirt, or him to scoop me up to carry me to the couch. But all he does is lift me so he can slide out from under me, returning to his cooking.

"Want to help?"

I do, and it's a good distraction.

***

I think about it for almost two weeks. Think about him. Think about the last day I saw Theo. Think about how he was dying, wasting away under whatever spell my father had used to make him like that. That even the moments we'd stolen years before—when he showed me how to defend myself, judging it a useful skill, when I'd helped at menial tasks so we could have a few moments together, when I'd pass on my lessons and we'd read together—were gone forever.

Theo was dying. Humans die, but he'd been so young and wasting away. A slow, cruel death.

And I'm glad he survived. The reality is that being upset is a waste of time. We can't change the past. I should have run with him, maybe.

But either way, it's not Theo's fault. And the urge to see him—to really know that he's okay, to see it with my own eyes—wins out.

Callum doesn't ask any questions when I tell him, which I appreciate more than I can say. He just pulls out his phone and texts Chase, who knocks on our door four hours later.

"That was quick," Callum says.

Chase grins, and I realize for the first time that his front teeth are sharper than I would expect them to be. "We're fast workers," is all he says, extending a paper.

"What is it?"

"An invitation. To a ball, a week and half from now. Technically it's for Celia and Bethany but you can go as their representatives."

I want to ask how he got it. Doesn't Bryce usually deal with those diplomatic matters? But then I think of the sharp teeth, the stories I've heard about Heath and Chase, and decide that maybe it's best not to ask.

Callum turns to me, the invitation in his hand. "What do you think, Marielle? Want to go to a ball?"

***

Bethany and Mae force me into the back of a car and drive four hours to find me a dress.

Bethany looks at me sympathetically in the mirror. "There's a lot of good parts of living so far from humans," she says. "But there's no decent shops. And we definitely don't have time to have a wolf custom make something for you. So, we have a ways to go to get something decent off the rack."

Mae's look is a lot less sympathetic. "Beauty takes work," she says. And sure enough, while Bethany is wearing the jeans and sweater I almost always see her in, comfortable and practical, Mae's outfit includes towering heels and a shirt with so many straps I couldn't possibly untangle them all.

So I've agreed to being in the car. I'm going to a vampire ball, a completely ludicrous statement. And not only will I see Theo for the first time in two hundred years—Theo, now mated to a vampire prince—but I'll also be representing all the wolves. Callum and I will be the first representatives the wolves have sent to the vampires in centuries. I need a dress, and a good one at that. And I gather that asking Chase to bring you to a primarily human town via his magic is generally forbidden. So, the car it is.

I realize about two hours into the drive that this is the longest I've been away from Callum, barring the nights he's left for the full moon. It shouldn't feel like such an empty ache; it shouldn't hurt. We'll be back very late tonight, and I won't even sleep anywhere but our bed. It still leaves something in me feeling empty, and I find my hand twitching, as if I'm reaching for him constantly.

"Don't you miss your mates?" I ask them, hoping I'm at least not alone.

Bethany chuckles lightly. "Gods, I remember those early days."

Mae looks a little more tense than Bethany's light laughter.

"Early days?"

Bethany tilts her head, considering. "The mating bond, it's demanding at first, right? Like you can't live without them. Probably giving you both time to fall in love and build a strong partnership and all of that. It's been a while, but I remember feeling like I was being eaten whole by it."

"So it's not always like this?" I ask, considering. It will be nice to not feel like I'm missing a part of myself if I go away for the day, but I've also gotten quite used to the way Callum and I drive each other a little mad, the way I can feel him just around the corner, the way I feel warmer when he's there, the way it's like we're sharing oxygen, thoughts.

The way he looks at me, like watching me is his greatest joy, will that go away?

"I've been mated to Celia for a thousand years almost," Bethany says. "No one would ever get anything done if it was always like that. It's incredibly intense at first. At least, I can only speak of my end, because I'm a wolf too. I don't know what you all feel."

"It's just as intense," Mae says shortly, and I wonder exactly how long early days include.

If you've been mated for a thousand years, what's a few decades, after all?

But Bethany looks at Mae with concern. "Still?"

Mae shrugs uncomfortably. "Bryce thinks we're making up for lost time or something. Because it took us so long to sort our shit out at the start, you know? But it could be a witch thing. We tend to be possessive over what we deem ours."

Bethany shrugs. "Maybe. It comes in waves, you know."

"Waves?" I can't help but ask.

"The mating bond will guide a wolf and what they need. Sometimes it feels like it starts all over again, in a way. Except you know each other now, every little thing and it's just frenzy. Devotion." She looks sideways. "I can't guarantee how that'll feel on your end, but I've watched Chase and Heath enough to get a feeling. Chase feels it too."

Frenzy. Devotion. Is that what I'm feeling right now?

Yes, I think. But also safety and home and something else, something soft and easy that I've never felt before, never even imagined before.

I shift in my seat. Today is going to be a long day.

CHAPTER THIRTY-FOUR

CALLUM

I pace our living room for the thousandth time. Most of my mind is consumed with the thoughts of what's coming next tonight.

Vampires and werewolves have a history of bitter disagreements. Of a long-held almost-hatred. In recent millennia, we've solved the problem by simply never interacting. I don't know how Heath and Chase got the invitation for Celia and I'll never ask. Certainly Bryce would have needed to work harder to do it through official channels. I don't think Celia has ever attended an event at vampire court, not once in a millennium.

There's no question of us not going, and I'm not going to mention any of this to Marielle. She wants to see her brother, deserves to know everything she wants about him and his life since the last time she saw him. And I hope he's happy and well and had no idea what fate had befallen her, and that she can forgive him for leaving her behind.

Marielle will always, always have a family with me. But I want her to have more people. She deserves it.

Wolves are all about packs and bonds. When mates bond, it's like just making a bigger family. Bethany's family is my family. Even Ryder and Hannah, or Mae's witchy friends, as little as she sees them these days. The wolf considers them all distant pack, extended family in a way. And it's a damn shame that Marielle didn't get to bring any of her own people into our pack. I want to give her her brother back.

Right now, though, Bethany, Mae, and Celia are working together to help her get ready for tonight's event. Celia isn't much for this type of thing. I suppose the event invitation was originally made out to her simply because she's the queen, but truth be told, Celia has always been more comfortable in an office or on a battlefield than in a ballroom.

But she's helping Marielle now, because Marielle is family, and I make a note to remember to thank my sister and my sisters by fate later for making this happen for Marielle.

Truth be told, I owe my entire family a thank you. Heath and Chase got the invitations. Mae, Celia, and Bethany got Marielle ready. And Bryce is sitting on my sofa, one eyebrow raised as he watches me pace, after making sure I am ready to diplomatically represent our people tonight.

Tonight is for Marielle, but I wish Bryce every future success with his diplomatic efforts. He can certainly keep them; it's nerve-wracking in the extreme. I'd much rather face an enemy with my fists than my words.

"I hope you have a better game face when you're in front of them," Bryce says.

"Shut the fuck up."

"And don't say shit like that."

"Fuck you."

Bryce just makes a tsking sound, and it's only centuries of practice that I can tell he's mostly just doing it to take the piss out of me.

"Remember, brother, you want them to like you."

"What's your excuse then?" I ask, mostly to be contrary, but then again, it's a question we've all asked at one time or another.

There are footsteps on the stairs, and I whirl to watch. It's just Mae, though.

She sees my shoulders slump. "No need to look so disappointed," she teases, then goes straight to her mate, sliding into his lap, running her hands up his chest and over his shoulders. He immediately puts an arm around her waist, pulling her to him.

"Almost ready?"

"Any second now."

Sure enough, there are footsteps on the stairs again, and this time it's Marielle, resplendent and beautiful and walking down the stairs towards me like she's the angel humans long ago mistook her mother's people for.

The dress is mostly black, but as I drag my eyes over her body, feasting on the sight, I see the silver stars stitched in. My mate is the night sky, her beautiful curves wrapped in the sky I long to hold her under.

If it's a taunt from my sisters by fate, teasing me for not fucking her under the moon yet, I'll take it. She looks delicious like this, the fabric of the bodice clinging to her curves before it flows down past her waist, trailing her like a silken waterfall.

I want to fall to my knees and find my way under that skirt. I want to kiss her and muss up the elaborate twist her hair is pinned into.

But more than anything, I want to dance with her, hold her close and watch that skirt flow when she moves, watch her eyes twinkle and feel her in my arms.

Why did I let Bryce berate me about court politics when I could have made him remind me how to dance? What a waste of resources.

She comes to a stop in front of me. "Do you like it?"

"You're beautiful, Marielle." Does my voice sound hoarse to other people too? "I've never seen anything lovelier." Her without any clothes at all, perhaps, because every version of Marielle is the most beautiful thing I've ever seen. But there's something about the way she's carrying herself in this dress that makes my mouth water.

I fiddle with the box in my hands, grateful for Bethany's instructions even when she wouldn't tell me what the dress looked like.

In the back of my mind, I process Celia ushering everyone out of the room. Hopefully, they're seeing themselves out of the house, giving us a moment of privacy, although I'm sure Chase is on his way over by now and will interrupt us soon enough.

"For you," I say, popping open the jewelry box to reveal what Bethany told me to purchase.

"They're beautiful," Marielle breathes, hesitant fingers reaching out to touch the box, then pulling them back.

"No, go on, they're yours."

She laughs disbelievingly. "Where did you even get these?"

"I bought them when you were dress shopping. Bethany gave me some hints on what would go with your dress. I wanted you to have something nice." I take the necklace from the box, setting the earrings in the box aside for now. "May I?"

She nods and half turns, giving me access to her neck.

I trail a reverent finger over the skin of her neck, from collarbone to just behind her ear, before I place the diamond necklace around her neck, clasping it in the back.

The silver chain is designed to look like a delicate trailing vine, to match my beautiful druidic mate. But each diamond, put where one might expect flowers, looks like stars in the sky.

The necklace sits close to her throat, and I congratulate myself for finding something that fits her dress perfectly.

The earrings took some effort, because she never had her ears pierced. But Bethany insisted I find some that clasp on.

It took some doing, but I found them, and they trail like twinkling stars from her ears, flashing against her neck as she turns her head to look at me, a red-painted smile so wide it makes my heart beat faster.

She turns again, the silver strands moving as she does, the diamonds at the end twinkling, the whole thing only highlighting the long line of her pointed-tipped ears.

"They're beautiful," she murmurs, raising a hand to gently touch the necklace.

It's on the tip of my tongue to offer to take her to a jewelry store, to offer to buy every single item that catches her eye. But something tells me that isn't the draw of this for her.

Her fingers drop from the necklace and reach for the vase of flowers she's taken to keeping on the end table. She takes out a red bloom, drooping slightly from the week or more it's been in the vase. Before my eyes, the bloom comes back to life, as if it was picked at just this very moment.

She steps closer to me, flower still in hand, eyes on my chest, and I go still under her hands while she smoothes my lapel and then pins the flower into place. She smoothes it out again once the flower is secure, and I can't stop watching it, can't stop watching her hands, fingernails now painted a deep, deep blue.

"There," she says lowly, still touching my chest. "Now you have something from me, too."

My mate, claiming me? Has any wolf ever been luckier?

"That I do," I murmur, my voice coming out huskily as she continues to touch my chest.

The flower feels like a brand against my chest, and I welcome it more than gladly. Can I get her to mark me forever?

"Gods, I want to kiss you," I tell her.

Her breath seems to catch. "Why don't you?"

I let one finger gently, reverently, chase the line of her jaw. "Because I'll make a mess of all this hard work. And because we'd be late." As if on cue, Chase knocks.

He lets himself in. "Ready to go?" he asks. "I don't have all night."

I step away from Marielle, but take her hand in mine, and turn to Chase, ready to see what tonight has for us.

CHAPTER THIRTY-FIVE

MARIELLE

The way Callum looks at me when I come down the stairs makes it all worth it. The drive, the dozens of dresses I tried on, the hours getting ready today—worth it.

Chase drops us at the base of a hill, on top of which sits a rather large castle. "As close as I can get, I'm afraid," he says. "They definitely know a thing or two about keeping visitors out. Come back down this far and call me when you're ready to go." And with that, he's gone once more.

Callum looks at me. "Can you walk up the hill?"

The shoes are definitely not conducive to climbing hills. "We'll see."

He squeezes my hand. "Happy to carry you. Just let me know if your shoes bother you." His eyes dart downward, and then he shakes his head. "Never knew I'd have an opinion on shoes."

"Oh?" I stick one of the shoes, silver and strappy, out from under the hem of my dress for us both to look at it. "And what's your opinion?"

He opens his mouth to say something, thinks better of it, and closes his mouth to think. "Impractical as all hell, but suddenly I find myself not minding so much." He smiles and leans over to kiss the top of my head. "They don't make you that much taller, though."

Not everyone can be a giant like all wolves apparently are. I don't voice that. "It took a while to find the shoes," I say.

"Oh yeah? You guys were gone for a while."

"Mhm. Dress took the most time. Shoes took a bit. Not as long as..."

"As?" he prompts.

I blush but decide to be brave. I brought it up for a reason, after all. "You should see what I'm wearing under the dress."

He grinds to a halt on the path, turning fully to face me. His face twists, and it looks almost painful. "You're telling me this now?" he demands, voice strangled.

"What? You don't want to know?"

"Not when I can't do anything about it," he says, and he steps closer to me, sliding his hands around my hips, dragging them lower, as if he'll be able to feel the lace underneath through all the material of the dress. "Gods, Marielle, I'll be thinking about that all night long."

"Good."

"Good? I'm supposed to make a good impression on the vampires tonight."

I laugh at his expression. "We'll do that. I'll see Theo again. And when we go home..." I trail off, my mind going back to what I thought of in the dressing room of that store Mae had dragged me into, blushing all the while. When we go home, he can help me with the zipper on my dress, and then I'll show him what's hiding underneath. And he can take it off slowly, and push me back on the bed, and we can...

I want him. No more waiting. If I can be brave enough to face my past, I can be brave enough to start this next part of my future.

Besides, the full moon is soon, and I'm determined to be ready for this one.

His eyes are dark, and whatever he's thinking, I think I like it. I shiver under his gaze, stepping somehow even closer into the circle of his arms.

"You'll have me well and truly distracted this whole party," he growls, squeezing me for a moment before stepping away, just taking my hand back in his. "Let's go."

***

The palace on top of the hill looks even grander up close.

If Theo is really living here, if Theo is really a prince here, then his life has been good indeed.

The vampire at the door studies our invitation carefully, looking us over with raised eyebrows. "You are not the werewolf queen."

"Callum Crae and my mate, Marielle," Callum says, smiling a charming smile I never see on him, something so fake and it looks like it hurts his face a bit. "I'm here on behalf of my sister."

He continues to stare at us, and I wonder if he'll deny us entry. Maybe I should say something, mention Theo, but something tells me it won't matter.

"Enjoy your evening," he says at last, apparently deciding there's no good reason to reject us.

Callum looks like he's biting back some sort of comment, so I just nod and tug on his hand, leading him into the grand ballroom.

I've never seen anything like this in my entire life. I've certainly never been to a party like this, and I've never seen so much opulent wealth on display.

The ballroom is huge, filled with all sorts of people, brightly colored dresses flashing as people dance. A string quartet plays in one corner, and the music echoes around the elaborate marble room. Rich tapestries and art that is probably quite expensive decorate the walls.

The Craes have money, and their homes are nice. But their homes are nice in a comfortable way.

I could never imagine living in a castle.

The one thing there doesn't seem to be any of at this party is food, although it's not hard to think of why. I resist raising a hand to my throat, wondering if they see us as food.

Callum finishes giving the place a look-over at the same time I do. "You'll get me to one party this fancy a century," he warns me, which honestly sounds more than good enough to me. "So we might as well enjoy it while we're here. Shall we dance until you spot your brother?"

I look around the room, but don't see him, so I nod, and Callum gives a little bow, holding his hand out for me to take.

I take it, and he whirls me onto the dance floor.

***

The whole room knows the moment Theo shows up.

The room goes quiet, and the music stops. The doors to the back—at least twenty feet tall, impractical and imposing all at once—open with a rather menacing creak.

Anyone stepping out of those doors should seem small by comparison, but not the couple who walks through. I know who the one on the left is without asking. Silas Emrick. The vampire prince.

He's tall, although probably not as tall as Callum. His blond hair is long and slicked back, covered on top by a crown dripping in jewels. With a sharp, angular face and hungry eyes, I would never look at him and think he's anything but vampire.

To his right is undoubtedly Theo. Theo, healthy now. His body filled out, healthy muscle covering his bones. Where Silas' features are sharp enough to cut a person, Theo's have fleshed out, the prior hunger erased from them.

If I thought Silas' crown was gaudy, Theo's certainly puts it to shame. The sparkling rubies catch the low light around the ballroom with every step he takes, the gold burnished to an impossible shine. It looks heavy, but Theo wears it well.

But underneath that—underneath the new health and the new wealth—he's still obviously Theo.

A Theo who holds hands with a vampire prince who surveys the room casually, before waving his free hand negligently. "Carry on," he says, and the band strikes back up.

Sudden nerves grip me. Should I go up to them? Would that be deemed rude, or bad manners, or even threatening?

Does he want to see me? Will I offend him? Worse, I'm not just here representing myself. I'm here as Callum's mate, and we're representing all the wolves, and if I make a fool of myself, it will reflect on them all.

I can't do that to them. Can't embarrass the people who have been so kind to me.

Bethany lent me her own makeup for tonight, since she's the only one as pale as me. Chase and Heath found Theo and got me this invitation. Bryce talked Callum through the diplomacy aspect. Mae taught me to walk in the shoes. And Celia, the queen I'm here to represent, did up the zipper on my dress herself.

Callum is clearly not having the same inner turmoil. He squeezes my hand. "You ready?"

I swallow. Am I? How should I do this? How does anyone do this, approach someone you haven't seen in two centuries?

He has Silas now. Maybe he's forgotten me, a remnant of a miserable human life best forgotten.

Callum squeezes my hand again. "C'mon. You won't know until you see him. And worrying'll do you no good."

I sigh. He's right, so I squeeze his hand back and lead the way through the dancers to where Silas and Theo are still standing.

There's a crowd forming loosely around them. They're not precisely in conversation with Theo and Silas, but it's as if people want to be close to them, to feel like they're involved. I stop, not wanting to join that crowd, but Callum just uses his bulk to push our way through.

He stops just short of them and gives a short bow, as much as a werewolf prince would give for courtesy's sake, I suppose. "Emrick."

Silas Emrick studies Callum's face with cold, hungry gray eyes. "Crae, I presume?"

"That's me."

He continues to study Callum and continues to hold Theo's hand. I wait with bated breath behind Callum, not wanting to burst into the interaction.

"Half my advisors have been in a tizzy about what the Craes could possibly want with us now," he says. "I expected to see your sister. Or at least your brother."

"I have a personal stake in this."

"Oh? Do tell."

Callum steps to the side and reaches for my hand. "My mate. Marielle."

I half notice Silas give a little start, but I have eyes only for Theo.

Theo, who clearly recognizes me despite the dress and the makeup and the years, whose eyes go wide and who takes a little involuntary step towards me. "It's you," he breathes.

Is that a good or bad thing? I can't tell, but I nod anyway, my earrings brushing my neck as I do. They remind me of Callum, and his hand still in mine. I stand a little straighter. "It's me. And it's you."

Theo steps all the way up to me. I don't miss how Silas and Callum both tense at that, but I hardly care. "You're here."

"I'm here."

He raises a hand but doesn't touch me, letting it fall. "Where have you been all these years?"

I swallow. "Did you look for me?"

"Yes. Gods, Marielle, yes, of course, Silas and I—but then your father was dead and there was no word of you and—"

"It's a long, miserable story," I say. My free hand goes to my stomach, just thinking of it. "But I'm free now. With my mate. And here."

Silas clears his throat. "Perhaps we should go somewhere to talk." He looks over the ballroom, frowning for a moment. "I'm sure our guests can entertain themselves for a bit."

CHAPTER THIRTY-SIX

MARIELLE

The sitting room Theo and Silas show us is much simpler than the ballroom. I sit on a couch as close to Callum as I can manage without being properly in his lap, and he puts a hand on my knee, letting me feel the heat of it even through my dress.

Silas and Theo settle on the opposite couch. "Where have you been for two centuries?" Silas says, breaking the silence.

His words don't sound kind, and I feel Callum tense beside me, but I try not to let it get to me.

Maybe Theo tried to come back for me. Maybe he thought I abandoned him. Maybe...

"I was sold," I say bluntly, looking just at Theo. "By my father."

Theo hisses, a sound ancient and terrible and obviously vampiric, and Callum's back goes ramrod straight, and something inside me tightens, as if I should be ready to fight.

It's not directed at me, though. Silas takes Theo's hand and strokes it, his thumb moving gently over the back of his hand, trying to soothe him.

"That bastard," Theo snarls. "We should have killed him."

"Don't think I didn't consider it," Silas says darkly. "I was simply too late."

"I thought he was going to marry you to someone, probably someone awful," Theo says, turning back to me. "Not..."

I shrug. "Halfling parts are apparently a spell commodity."

I don't try to describe what happened. I don't want to think about it, don't want to talk about it. Don't think anyone in this room needs to hear it, not when even Silas shudders at the implication behind what I already said.

"How long?"

"Until a couple of months ago," I murmur. "Callum saved me."

Saved me. To put it mildly. He pulled me out of there, then gave me a chance at life I never thought I'd have. I'm free.

"I thought you were dead," I say to Theo. "I assumed—you didn't tell me about Silas."

"No," he agrees softly. "I didn't. I didn't—I thought the less you knew the better. I'm sorry, Marielle."

I'm sorry. And I'm sorry too. For the centuries, for what happened during my childhood.

"We can start fresh now," I offer.

Theo smiles. "I'd like that. You and your mate are welcome here anytime, Marielle."

I look sidelong at Silas, as though he, the prince, might contradict such a generous offer to a wolf and his mate. But Silas isn't looking at me. He's looking at Theo with undisguised fondness, and he doesn't say a word.

***

Silas and Theo need to return to their own party. "You know how politics are," Theo says, although truth be told, I don't, really. Maybe I should set about learning.

Theo hugs me before they leave, and I lean into it. "I'll see you again before you leave, sister," he whispers. "And as often as we can after that. Promise me."

Sister. "I promise."

He glides away with his mate, leaving Callum and me behind at that over-large door. Callum chuckles, taking my hand again, and pulling me close. "It worked out then."

"It did," I say, half-marveling at it still. His arms come up to encircle me, pressing me to him, and he rubs his hands along my bare arms. "What are you doing?"

"Wolf doesn't like that you smell like a vampire," he mutters. "So I'm fixing it."

I'm half-tempted to talk about the other ways we can change my scent—the things we should go home to do—when Callum stiffens.

"What is it?" I ask.

"Not sure," he murmurs. "Smells like..." He takes a very obvious sniff, then guides me around the ballroom. He looks like a bloodhound with a scent, but I don't stop him, waiting for him to find whatever he's looking for.

He stops at the far end, by the door, and it doesn't take long to see what's drawn his attention.

CHAPTER THIRTY-SEVEN

MARIELLE

Divine.

I've never seen the divine before, but I know without asking, without whatever scent clearly drew Callum here.

She's as small as I am, but her presence makes her seem ten feet tall. There's just something about her—an aura maybe—that takes up the entire room.

And her pointed ears, absolutely dripping in jewelry, are a dead giveaway.

I freeze in place, not sure if I want to keep going or not.

As if in support, Callum wraps an arm around me, squeezing me lightly. Telling me the choice is mine.

But it's not, because she turns to us then, probably feeling our gaze.

She's dancing with a vampire, her hands and eyes on him in a way that makes me wonder for a quick second about my parents' own ill-fated courtship. But she looks me over, one long sweeping look, and breaks away from the vampire without a second glance.

I don't think I breathe as she walks over to me. "You are Rota's," she says, her voice hypnotically deep.

I blink. "What?"

"Rota. Your mother is Rota."

"I have no idea who my mother was," I tell her.

"Is. Your mother is Rota. I'd recognize your face anywhere. You look like Rota."

Well, I certainly never looked like my father. "How do you know my mother?"

"She's my sister. For ten thousand years, she's been my sister. I know her better than anyone else."

I swallow. An aunt. Family. I could make out with a wealth of family today. Callum's family who has accepted me so completely, my brother finally back in my life, and an aunt.

But as she watches me with her cold eyes, I remember it's been two centuries.

I reach up to touch Callum's hand, currently across my stomach. He squeezes me reassuringly in response.

"Tell me about her then," I challenge.

Her lip curls. "What is there to say? Ten thousand years ago, a god of night had seven daughters. Your mother was one of them. I see you hold her same affinity for the night sky," she says, sparing barely a glance for Callum.

I flush at her implication.

"How about saying why she abandoned her kid for two centuries?" Callum says, voice dripping with disdain.

Her icy stare turns to actually look at him now. It's not just cold in appearance, either. I literally feel cold, a shiver wracking through me I can't suppress. I want to get her gaze off of him, want to step between them. "Don't interfere in things you don't understand, wolf."

"He understands me," I say, proud that my voice doesn't break. "He understands me and he's my family. And he has every right to be a part of this conversation."

"He's your family?" she asks mockingly.

"Why, were you going to claim me?" I challenge her. Because she won't. Because Rota and her sister left me to flounder for two centuries.

They could have protected me in a thousand different ways. But they didn't.

The vampire she was dancing with clears his throat, taking a step forward. "Es—"

154

"Not now," she snaps, waving him back without even turning around. Then she steps closer to me, the chill becoming even more pronounced. Her eyes feel like ice, and with every step closer she takes, I feel like they're pinning me in place.

"You're a curious thing, niece," she says.

Curious, like an animal. Like a pet.

I turn away from her, breaking her icy stare, and turn to Callum. "I'm done here."

He looks only at me, although I don't doubt that a great deal of his attention is on the ice-eyed woman in front of us. "Sounds good, Marielle. Let's go."

"Do you want answers or not?" my aunt asks, voice clipped.

"I'm alright," I tell her, still looking only at Callum. Let her be ignored for once. "You and your family mean nothing to me."

Callum smiles softly. He wraps his arm tighter around me as the chill in the air gets worse, and he starts to turn us, as if he'll stand between me and her if she attacks.

Then something seems to happen, and the unnatural coldness fades. My aunt steps back to the vampire who's been waiting for her. Half of me wants to warn him, wants to tell him I'm the consequence of how relationships with the divine end.

Me. Hannah. How many of us are there? Do I have half-siblings?

"My mistake," she says, and her tone is cold even as the chill has left the air. "I'll leave you to your life then, niece."

She walks away, and I can't help watching her as she takes her vampire by the hand and leads him away.

"She didn't even tell us her name," Callum says.

Probably not an oversight.

"C'mon," I mutter, suddenly tired and still very cold. "I'm done with this."

CHAPTER THIRTY-EIGHT

CALLUM

Marielle sighs and then removes herself from my arms. I almost protest letting her go, but she manages to give me a small smile. "Think I can do that thing? With the cold?"

Could my Marielle ever be cold? Unlikely. She is so warm and bright, and I would never think of a single thing about her being cold. I doubt she's capable of it.

But as far as the larger question goes—"Wouldn't be surprised if you had some talents you haven't tapped into yet." I've seen her, after all, and what she can do with the energy from plants. I've seen her heal herself with just a tree.

Her hand goes to her stomach, and my own stomach drops in response. Right. Whatever mystical gifts being a halfling gives her, her captors knew far more about it than either of us do. And they carved her up over it.

"What do you say we get out of here?" I ask her, taking the hand not on her stomach. "Say goodbye to Theo and just go home?"

Maybe if we leave now, she'll remember this night for the reunion with her brother, and not for how it ended.

She tilts her head to consider it, then nods. "Alright then. Where'd Theo and Silas get to?"

They're not hard to spot; if you couldn't see the crowd parting around them, the shiny, gaudy jewels would give them away. Damn vampires.

But I bury the thought for Marielle's sake. Vampiric brother by fate. I can manage it. For Marielle, I'll happily manage it.

Marielle leads us over to them. Theo and Silas are more reserved in front of the crowd, but Theo still squeezes Marielle's hand and extracts a promise that she'll come back within the month.

Then the crowd parts for us, and, still hand in hand, we walk out.

***

The first thing I do is loosen the damn tie. Marielle giggles. "Not a fan?"

"Hate the damn thing." I look her over, still moving along in those sharp shoes. "How are you holding up?"

She shrugs. "Looking forward to getting out of all this."

Well, that certainly changes the direction of my thoughts, and I remember what she told me earlier. *You should see what I'm wearing underneath it.*

Damn.

Now I can't think of anything else, and I'm half tempted to pick her up so we can run down the hill, calling Chase's name the whole way, just to get home sooner.

What's underneath that dress?

Will she let me see it tonight?

She smiles up at me, like she knows exactly where my thoughts have gone. I watch her, the smile mostly daring, teasing. But I'd have to be blind not to see the tremor underneath it, and I'm never blind to my Marielle.

"Marielle, are you sure you want..." I trail off, because she's already shaking her head. "Marielle. There's no time pressure here. I promise. No judgment. You've been hurt and I don't ever want you to be scared."

She takes my hand, still in hers, and places it over her belly. "I got hurt," she agrees. "A lot. And you know what? When I remember it, I think of them carving open my belly. Or when they pulled out my heart one time. Or the darkness, every day. What happened, the way they touched me… the rape… I remember it, but not more than anything else." Her eyes close, then open again. "I'm nervous because this feels important for us. And yes, I don't know what I'm doing. But it's not what you're worried about."

I study her face, then use my hand on her stomach to stroke her skin there. "Alright, Marielle," I breathe. I cup her face in my free hand. "I want. Trust me, I want. If you're unsure or uncomfortable, you'll tell me to stop, right?"

She smiles at me, but before she can make the promise, a concussive burst goes off, and we go flying.

Chapter Thirty-Nine

Marielle

I wake up alone.

I know I'm alone, even without opening my eyes. It's like I can always feel Callum now, can feel his presence, and now all I feel is the absence of it.

I try to open my eyes, to look around, but it doesn't work. That sets off a round of panic, and I squirm and fight as if I must really still be chained up on that floor, blinded and left to rot except for when they wanted to carve me up.

But no. I can move, and I take comfort from that while I wait for my vision to come back.

It must have been a hell of a hit to the head. I stick my hand into the dirt, trying to call the energy of the earth to heal me, and feel it, a sharp spike of adrenaline, then a soothing, warm blanket enveloping me.

I try to take stock of what happened. Callum and I were leaving. We had met my aunt, and I wanted to be anywhere else. I'd promised Theo I'd see him again soon. And Callum and I were talking about the rest of the night.

And then... nothing.

My vision comes back soon enough, and I blink around. No Callum.

Who would take him? Who could?

Callum is fierce strength, centuries of training, and the beast that lurks inside of him. Who could possibly take him?

My mind goes to my supposed aunt, who I never even got the name of. With the power we'd glimpsed inside her, just a glimpse being enough to set my teeth on edge...

But no. Why would she be so interested in Callum? She hadn't wanted either of us.

But it's that thought that makes it clear. Me. It's me. I'm here, relatively safe, given the circumstances. And that is the only thing that could ever give someone an advantage over Callum.

Fuck. Fuck. I need to... I need to...

I need to get it together. I couldn't do anything centuries ago when I was captured. I was mortal, I was drugged, I was unprepared and surprised and alone.

The only one of those things I still am is surprised, and it's wearing off fast.

"Chase... Crae," I grunt out, remembering the conversation I had with Heath. His true name. Call him and he'll come. Family.

Nothing.

I wait and wait, my strength returning, but no sign of Chase. Am I alone after all? Again?

Or, I realize with the slowly dawning clarity of a serious head injury fading, am I just not far enough down the damn hill?

Stuck in some sort of limbo, between the vampire prince and his consort's awareness and the notice of my new family?

I force myself to my feet, but only make it a step or two before I fall. I growl and unstrap the damn heels. Callum was right about their impracticality, even if he'd also admitted to liking how they look.

I push back to my feet and manage a few more steps, still wobbling but at least no longer balancing on knife points. And I start chanting Chase's name, hoping, hoping, that this step will be the one, that now—

"I heard you the first time, gods—Marielle, what the hell?" he snaps, and steps from my side into my field of admittedly still blurrier-than-I'd-like vision.

"Someone... someone attacked us," I manage, and then I lose my footing again, and Chase catches me, and we're gone before I know what's going on.

Chase's required energy payment all but knocks me back to unconsciousness, so I'm unable to walk as he hauls me up the front steps to Celia's house, shouting the whole time.

Bethany reaches us first, helping him to guide me to a couch in their living room, and I frown, knowing I'm covered in dirt. They don't seem to care, their low voices beginning to speak, all but ignoring me.

Celia joins them next, her voice deeper than her mate's, her tone rougher. She comes by me and squeezes my shoulder, and the gesture hurts even as I know it wasn't intended to.

Then I hear Mae. "What the fuck is wrong with her?" she demands.

The room goes silent. "She already looks better than when I found her," Chase decides, and he's right. I feel better.

Better being a relative term. I'm still not convinced I could stand.

But if there's one thing I know about myself, it's that I heal fast.

Mae's hand grips my chin, tilting me to look at her. "Marielle. Marielle. Focus on me."

I try. The edges still seem fuzzy.

"Listen, I have something that will perk you up a bit. Bit like a magical stimulant. You'll crash hard later, but it'll help us sort this all out faster, alright?"

"And why do you have that?" I hear Bryce mutter, but I ignore him, already nodding.

Bethany gets Mae a glass of water and Mae stirs in some sickly green powder, then tilts the whole concoction down my throat. "There. Perfect."

It hits me like I got dropped off a cliff or something, the sudden adrenaline rush knocking into me so fast I feel like I fly out of my skin. I cough. "We need to talk about what's in that," I mutter, thinking about the plants involved before I force my thoughts back to a more useful track.

"What happened, Marielle? Was it the vampires?" Celia's voice is no nonsense. No sign she's in any way freaked out, except in her eyes.

161

"No, they were... Theo and Silas were kind to us," I say. "I don't know what happened. I don't know who did it. There were a lot of people there. There was at least one divine there. My aunt, apparently. Vampires, a few witches, definitely a siren or two, some sorcerers I think; pretty much any group you could think of. We were leaving. And I have no idea who did this to us. But they took him."

Mae's enchanted energy booster must be a really powerful enchantment, because the panic doesn't debilitate me this time.

"Any idea who?" Heath asks, stepping more clearly into my view. "Anything at all?"

I shake my head. I didn't see anything. Didn't even sense the attack coming. Callum might have. But I'd distracted him.

"There was an explosion," I say, trying to piece together what I could. "We weren't paying attention, just talking as we walked. And then there was an explosion and..."

"An explosion?" Bryce pushes.

I shrug. "I remember getting tossed into the air. A bright light, maybe. And that was it. I was unconscious, and when I woke up, Callum wasn't there."

There's a stiffness in the room. "Look at her," Chase says tightly to the family. "She's healed almost entirely. Faster than any of us here. The time between her being unconscious and waking? They didn't have much time."

"It must have been a hell of a blast to knock Callum out," Bryce says. "Bastard is hard-headed and can take a hit. If it knocked him down, it wouldn't be for long."

"Who would want to take Callum?" Bethany asks.

"Lots of groups," Heath says. "Revenge, on him or on us."

"Take him and leave her?" Bethany asks doubtfully.

Chase sighs. "Mae, come with me. We're going to go see if there's anything left of what they used. Two casters are better than one."

Heath frowns. "You're not going to vampire territory alone. We still can't rule them out."

I open my mouth to defend Theo, but Heath is gone, going upstairs. He comes back moments later with a sword. "I'm borrowing this," he says to his sister, who just waves him off.

Then, before I can say anything, Heath reaches out for Chase, who reaches out for Mae, and the three of them disappear.

Bryce growls, low and fierce, and begins to pace, but Bethany and Celia ignore him. "Can you stand, do you think?" Bethany asks me.

I should try. I still feel fuzzy around the edges, but from what the others are saying, I've physically healed up. I let her haul me to my feet, and take a few steps, more steady now. "Do you have anything I could wear?" I ask, not wanting the dress Callum so admired. Not now.

Bethany's lip purses. Nothing that will fit me, I realize, and no one is willing to waste time going to the other houses. Not even Heath to get his own weapon.

So in this over-the-top dress, I wait. I wait for news, for an answer, for my mate.

Chapter Forty

Callum

The explosion doesn't knock me out for long. Maybe they mistimed it. Maybe they underestimated what a thousand years of training can do to a wolf.

Maybe they just underestimated the wolf, because I've never felt the creature so close to fully taking over, clawing under my skin as I snap awake.

Mate. Protect.

I'm more beast than man, my mind fully focused on Marielle and her safety. A quick glance tells me she's unconscious.

The wolf roars at the thought, impotent and useless, but that's okay. I can put him to better use.

I tear my eyes away from Marielle to see our attackers. Casters. An entire contingent of them, magic sparking between their fingers. They're a motley group, and I can sense warlocks and witches and demons intermixed.

They smell familiar.

It's the scent of pain and misery that lingered on Marielle when she first came home to us, I realize, my stomach dropping at the thought. The wolf pushes again, insisting on taking hold, but I hold him back. I'm better with the warrior, not the beast, in control.

I'm better for Marielle this way, I think, and that thought is the only thing that lets the beast grudgingly yield control to me.

I didn't bring any weapons tonight, but I hardly need them. I'm a wolf, and a well-trained one at that, and the wolf knows full well that our mate is on the line and I swipe with claws and teeth from the beast.

I taste blood, feel it on my skin, but I don't stop. It's a familiar feeling, and right now, to the wolf, to me, it is right. We should be covered in blood. Someone has hurt us. Someone has threatened our mate.

I step over a body, making my way towards another one. Target, I think, obstacle.

Prey, the wolf thinks as I wrap my hand around their throat, ready to tear them into pieces.

"I wouldn't," a voice threatens, and I turn to look.

The demon is standing over Marielle, who is still unconscious. He holds a sword to her neck.

I freeze, and the wolf growls, more deep and menacing than I've ever heard it.

I know Marielle has been hurt in imaginable ways. She's suffered more injuries than almost any immortal I know, even the most battle-hardened of us. And she's survived.

But even a divine halfling won't survive her head being removed from her shoulders.

"What do you want?" I don't recognize my own voice, the deep growl permeating every word.

There's a silence so long that I want to lash out. But that damned sword keeps me in place.

"Take the damn girl," one of them snaps. The one in my hands squeaks, and the only thing that stops me from throttling him is the keen eyes of the one with the sword.

"Honestly? We didn't anticipate the wolf waking. But you'll make a good enough consolation prize. And who knows. Maybe she'll be stupid and come after you."

Consolation prize. So they came to get Marielle back.

165

It makes sense, and I curse myself for not having planned for it, for being so arrogant that I thought we got them all. Marielle made them money. Marielle's body apparently made them spells beyond normal comprehension.

And I hadn't protected her.

"I won't let you touch her," I growl, itching to remove that sword from her neck, not knowing how. I'm fast, but even I'm not that fast.

"Wolves," one of them says, like it's a curse.

"I know you won't," the one with the sword says. "Because you'll come with us to ensure we don't hurt her, hm?"

I try to think of a way around it, try to think, try to see—anything, at this point, anything I can do—

He lets the sword dig into her neck, and for the first time in my very long life, the wolf rips out of me, swallowing my soul.

Chapter Forty-One

Marielle

I pace Celia and Bethany's living room with Bryce until the others finally return. At least my steps are steady now.

I curl my hand into a fist. Some comfort.

At last, they appear back into the living room, Mae stumbling out of Chase's grip and towards a waiting Bryce, who picks her up by her thighs so he can bury his face in her hair.

Heath has a paper clutched in one hand. "Six dead warlocks. They smell like the ones from the night we found Marielle," he says, handing the paper to his sister.

Celia skims it before passing it to me, and I frantically take it in.

We have the wolf. Halfling, if you want your pet back, you'll find us at the manor. Come before the full moon, and come prepared to bargain.

I look up grimly, looking at Celia, who is looking back at me unblinking while Bryce rips the note from my hand.

***

I don't let the idea of whether I should go turn into an argument. It is not a question of should. I will be going.

Arguments about strategy and plans follow me as I retreat to Callum's and my home, as I slip upstairs to change into clothes more suited for a rescue, as I take out the knives Callum gave me, tucking one into the jeans under my sweater, and using the sheath I hadn't had an opportunity to test yet to put the other around my thigh.

The argument is still going on when I get downstairs, but Celia sees me before anyone else. "Enough," she says, and everyone quiets immediately. "Marielle. All plans will hinge on you. What are you willing to do?"

I swallow. Anything. Everything. Even the things I'm sure they want from me. Even that.

"I'm going to get him back," I say, and my voice is quiet, but I know every single one of them hears it. "And I'm going into that place alone."

Heath's mouth twists. "You sure? Marielle, I saw that place, remember."

"And now it's a burned-out husk," I remind him. "But it doesn't matter what you did or didn't see there. If they have Callum, and we don't look like we're meeting their demands, then..." I shudder. I won't think about it.

But the fact remains that I know exactly what they can do to a person. And maybe a werewolf's spleen isn't as useful to them as a halfling's, but I have every confidence they'd cut him open anyway, just to prove a point.

"What you do after I have him is up to you," I say, although I know it's more complicated than that.

Because I won't be walking out with him. I'll be lucky if they really let Callum go for me.

I don't say it. They're smart people and no doubt know this, and I don't want a debate. I'm going. That's final.

***

Chase takes us all to the ruined husk of a manor I was kept in for so long. The energy expended should be great, but Heath pays it.

I look at the manor, expecting to feel...something. Anything.

But, other than the deep sense of foreboding from my missing mate, I really don't feel anything. What does the outside of this mansion mean to me? I never saw it until it was already on fire.

The pain is all inside, but even that isn't tugging at me like I worried it might. I'm too consumed by thoughts of Callum. Of what they've done to him.

That's the trouble with immortals. We can survive so much, and that's both a blessing and a curse.

I look at Celia, but she's looking right back at me. Waiting for me, I realize, and even though she is queen—my queen, now—this is my mission. My choices.

"I'm going," I say. "Give me some time. And then do what you want. But don't let them see you."

I don't wait around to argue or debate. Callum is in there. And I will do whatever it takes to get him out.

I have two knives. I have the earth beneath my feet. And, hopefully, I'll have Callum.

The manor didn't burn completely, although most of it is gone. It's unclear where they might be keeping Callum in this mess, considering they'd need a lot to keep him down, like some sort of cell or chains.

Unless they're using pain. That can work too.

I cross to where the front door was, where the shell of the entryway still remains, more or less.

Something feels off the moment I walk inside, something evil, something dark. Something that makes my hair stand on end.

An arm grabs me from behind, a hand clamping over my mouth. And then I disappear into nothingness.

Chapter Forty-Two

Callum

I'm still here, even as the wolf leads.

When I lead, I can feel the wolf hovering underneath my skin, expressing opinions, ready to defend. Now, it feels like it's in reverse, like I'm the passenger, to be listened to or ignored as best suits the wolf.

I try not to be angry. It's not malice. The wolf isn't capable of it, not towards me. It's just protection.

I pace the cell they've stuck me in, mystically enforced. I tried ramming myself at the bars for hours, but I couldn't so much as touch them.

I've listened to them debate for what feels like hours now. One of them wants to cut me open right now, and I don't think the threat of my bared teeth is really working to dissuade him. He wants to experiment, to see how effective pieces of the wolf can be as spell ingredients.

The others hold him off, waiting for something. They want me for something worse, and I brace myself for it.

I try to force the wolf to let me go, to change back, but it refuses to release me. The threat is still there, the worry for Marielle—

I don't know what happened to her. I don't remember those first few minutes after the change, just that the wolf had definitely ripped out several more throats before the one with the sword to Marielle's neck had dug the blade in once more. And then the wolf had given up, the fight leaving us in an instant.

Our wolves only take over to defend us in the direst situations. And the only thing that wins out over our own lives, in the wolves' minds, is our family.

For our mate, my wolf would take any punishment.

A demon appears, not Chase, not Ryder, not any demon I've ever met. And in his arms is Marielle, struggling fiercely.

She makes no ground against him, though, and four of the warlocks step forward, chanting a spell in unison, until glowing cuffs appear on Marielle's arms and legs.

The demon releases her and shakes out his arms. "Hell-cat," he spits, then moves away from her, to the safe distance most of them stand at.

I growl, deep and menacing, but everyone but Marielle ignores me. She turns to me, eyes wide and filled with tears, which only sets us to growling again. The wolf and I agree we hate seeing her cry, that we'll fight and kill to stop it.

How'd they get her?

"Let him go," she says, and despite the tears, her voice doesn't shake. "That was the deal."

"Slow down there, halfling. Aren't you happy to be back here?"

Marielle tenses. "I came. You have me. Let him go."

She's too smart to think they're going to let me go. But she asks anyway.

"You know, There was a fair bet you'd miss the full moon deadline, and we'd get to keep him. Already in his wolf form, and with the added vulnerability of the moon? Even considering the source of the ingredients is subpar, they could still hold a lot of power. And there's use for a wolf under your control."

"I'm here," Marielle repeats. "You have me."

One of them *tsks*. "You know the rules, halfling. You'll be chained and blinded."

I charge the bars again. Nothing.

She lifts her jaw defiantly. "Fine."

There's a heavy pause in the air, and a growl builds in me at the tension. "Show us you mean it. Do it yourself."

The growl rips from me, and I throw myself at the bars again and again. I want to beg her to leave. Want to beg her to run, to leave me behind. Try to tell the wolf that he's causing the problems, not protecting me, because I can't speak to my mate, can't tell her I'm not worth this, that I will happily stay here forever, die for her, let them cut pieces off of me, if it means she won't ever have to live through this again.

The wolf doesn't relent, just lunges at the bars again and again and again.

"Fine," Marielle says. "Give me a tool, then."

"You have fingernails, don't you?"

Marielle freezes and the wolf whines. But she nods, determinedly, and jerks her cuffed wrists. "Well?"

There's the chanting again, and the wolf tries to drown it out with his whining. It doesn't work.

CHAPTER FORTY-THREE

MARIELLE

The minute the demon lands, I know where we are.

I haven't been here in centuries, but it doesn't matter. This is my father's house.

I suppose he really is dead then, if his property has been taken over by these warlocks. Maybe they killed him. Maybe that's what he gets for thinking he could work with them, enslave a human, sell his daughter to them. Maybe this is justice.

The place doesn't look the same. My father's laboratory, once filled with potted plants and jars and careful weights and everything he needed for tinctures and tonics and poisons, now holds a cell with a large wolf, prowling back and forth.

Callum.

I swallow. He's transformed into the wolf, and my time in the village has told me how rare that is. And how dangerous.

He might not be much help then.

That's okay. I don't need help. They don't know it, but they have handed me everything I need.

I answered their letter with no plan except to rescue Callum. To make whatever trade necessary, to do whatever it takes. I had nothing on my side but two knives and a determination to succeed.

They might have changed my father's laboratory, but this was the house of a druid. And although they might think of me simply as a halfling, as an endless supply of spell ingredients, I'm half druid too.

Maybe my father will finally be good for something.

One of the chains loosens, just as one warlock steps up to Callum's cell with a lethal-looking spear. "Just so you don't get any ideas."

I need them to lower their guard. I need them to think I'm no threat.

I raise my hand to my eye.

Chapter Forty-Four

Callum

The wolf howls as she digs her fingernail into her eye, as her face scrunches in obvious pain, but she does it anyway. She doesn't make a single sound.

The wolf howls and howls and I scream inside, some mixture of her name and no and a desperate plea for her to leave.

We're ignored.

Chapter Forty-Five

Marielle

I try to ignore the pain, shoving it deep, deep down, to deal with later or never, really. When one eye is destroyed, I use the remaining one to look around, taking in the oddly flat world, where I can't quite get a grasp on it all.

But I can see enough. Enough to know that the man with the spear has let his attention slide to me, and not Callum.

That's all I need.

The plants my father grew in carefully labeled and cultivated pots are gone. It would be nice if they were still here, because some were incredibly poisonous.

But my father was a druid, and he was powerful in his own way. And one thing you can say about druids, is that plants can't help but grow around us. The very earth responds to our touch.

I felt it the moment I arrived. Under the floor, in the walls, in the dirt outside the house—they're everywhere. Waiting.

And I'm just the one to call it forward.

I might not have been able to do it if it weren't for Mae's magical energy booster. And spending it all in one big move like this probably means I'll crash right after.

That just means I only have one chance at this, one chance to get it right. That's fine. I expected that.

With one move of my hands, the plants burst forth, growing rapidly, striking out at my enemies. A sharp vine punctures one man through the chest. Another wraps around a neck, strangling a man. I turn my attention to the demon, tightening a vine around his throat until at last it severs the skin. No one is getting out of here tonight.

With one hand, I squeeze the plants tighter. With the other, I grab my knife.

Plants won't be enough. With immortality in play, best to be sure. The only thing to do is separate their heads from their bodies.

The poor vision is a nuisance, but I don't need perfect depth perception to cut, not when my target is held so still.

I twitch my hand around the knife handle. I've never killed anyone before. Theo taught me how to defend myself, but I never used it.

Callum's plaintive howls break through my concentration, and I cut.

Chapter Forty-Six

Callum

I t's the third one she cuts that does it.

Removing a head from the shoulders is messy business. The wolf could do it with his powerful jaw, probably, and as a man I've done it too many times, with swords and claws and teeth and anything else I can get my hands on.

Marielle's knife makes it difficult, and ugly, and it takes time. I wince at every cut, and she winces too, but she's determined.

The third one makes whatever spell they've put on the bars drop.

I can feel it, like a buzzing I didn't even know I could hear finally stopping, and I ram myself against the bars until they give, no match for the wolf.

And then it's all over. Marielle, who has done so much, who is starting to flag, doesn't need to worry anymore.

The wolf shows no mercy.

***

When it's over, when everyone in the room but Marielle and I are dead, I go to her side, urging the wolf to let me turn back.

It doesn't.

So I guide her into a chair, nudging her along with my nose.

She gives me a shaky smile, then falls into the chair.

I whine, wanting to stay with her, wanting to check her over, but I know there's more to do.

I let the wolf take over, taking off into the rest of the house, making sure that there's no one left alive to threaten my mate.

***

When I make it back to that damned basement, Marielle is asleep in the chair, looking dangerously close to tipping out of it.

Her face is covered in blood. Some of it is her own, some of it is from those she had to kill. Without conscious input from me, I lick it away.

Wolves.

I want my body back; I want my hands to hold her and my voice to speak to her and my damn brain to be running the show so I don't lick blood off of her.

But the wolf doesn't respond to my plea to let me take control again, ignoring it just like every other time since he took over.

Marielle blinks awake, my snout still inches from her face. Her hand comes up, still shaky, and her fingers lace in the fur at my neck. "Hello."

I touch her face with my nose, and she laughs slightly. "Wet nose. Okay. I can deal with this."

Gods, I don't want her to have to deal with this. It's humiliating.

But her fingers are tight in my fur, like she won't let me go. And I honestly think it's taking every last ounce of her strength to hold me, so I'll take it for what it is.

My mate, not letting me go. Four legs and all.

I look at her face critically. Her eye is a mess, and everything in me wants to look away, avoid it, but I can't. Because she did that for me. Would have plucked both of them out for me, gone into the darkness she spent two centuries in again, for me. So I can be brave enough to see it.

It's starting to heal, slowly. I don't know how long it will be until she has sight again. Maybe if she sleeps, she'll wake up healed. I can only hope.

She's not wounded other than that, not that I can see or smell. Just tired.

I can work with just tired.

I break her grip on my fur, disturbingly easy to do. Not that I think she'd really yank on my fur if I wanted to move—Marielle has never been harsh in her life—but it is disturbing to realize how weak her grip is.

Sleep. She needs sleep.

I want to speak. I want hands, arms to lift her, a chest to hold her to. All the things I took for granted before.

Instead, I nudge her to the floor and then curl up around her, letting her use me as a pillow.

She's out in minutes, and I keep as still as possible so I don't disturb her.

***

Eventually, I need to move from under her, and I hold my breath the whole time, but she doesn't wake. When I hurry back from defiling this manor by using a random corner to do my business—gods, being stuck as a wolf is humiliating—and from stealing whatever food I found upstairs, I lie down next to her again. And all she does is turn into me, seeking my warmth.

I prop my snout on the top of her head, whine softly, and just hope she wakes up soon.

***

On the second day, I wake up to Marielle's head on my stomach.

My naked stomach. My human stomach.

It seems the wolf has finally let me go, retreated into the back of my mind, curled up and content.

Our enemies are dead, I'm free, and my mate, healing and safe, is curled up on top of me. The wolf likely sees his job as done.

Marielle is still dead to the world, so I temper my excitement, simply moving a human hand down to run through her hair.

I'll never take hands for granted again.

Her hair is stiff with blood and dirt and I frown. Is it worth waking her up to try to find a way to clean her up?

She pushes into my hand, then rubs her face on my stomach, settling deeper into sleep, and I suppose I have my answer.

***

Two hours later, she wakes up. I can feel her breathing change, can hear her heart rate pick up, and I'm awake instantly, running my hands over her back and sides as soothingly as I can.

"What happened?" she asks fuzzily, voice muffled as she buries her head deeper in my chest. That seems to give her pause. "You turned back."

"Yeah," I say, stroking her hair. "We're safe now." But not for long. I'd been able to do some quick mental math while she slept, and the moon is coming up on us fast.

"Good," she says, sitting up to look around, and frowning. I move to follow her up, but catch the frown and, oh. Corpses.

Damn wolf, not thinking about things like that.

Then again, the wolf hadn't been in the best position to remove her from the situation. With human hands and arms, I'm in better shape.

She shudders. "I need to get out of here."

Right. Away from the corpses. I nod, sitting up. "We can call Chase from upstairs." Although I admit, I don't exactly have the firmest grasp on where the wolf dropped bodies upstairs.

She shakes her head rapidly. "No. Out of this house."

The shaking only intensifies, so I nod rapidly. "Alright, anything, anything you need," I try to soothe, pushing myself to my feet and offering her a hand that she quickly takes.

"Sorry," she whispers, like she has anything to apologize for. "I just never thought I'd be back here."

I look at her sidelong. "Did they keep you here?"

She sucks in a breath and turns to stare at me. "This is, or was, I guess, the house I grew up in. It's my father's house."

I feel my stomach drop out. Shit.

CHAPTER FORTY-SEVEN

MARIELLE

Before I know what's happening, he's scooped me into his arms and is speed-walking out of the house. I throw my arms around his neck.

"Callum, what on earth?"

"Gonna get you out of here," he mutters. "Right the fuck now."

Oh. Okay, then.

I don't really want to be here, either. Not with that damn cell he was kept in, not with the corpses. Not with the memories of my father lurking in the halls.

But Callum runs from the place like beasts are nipping at his heels.

Outside, the sun has just started to set, lighting the gardens—overgrown, weedy, neglected for centuries—a brilliant orange glow.

Over there was where Theo and I hid, where he taught me to fight and he told me what he remembered of his human life, before my father. And over there was the garden of poisonous plants that I'd tended with my father, the only time he ever seemed to really look at me.

"Call Chase," Callum says, voice raspy and interrupting my memories. "You need to go home."

I almost do, but then stop. "I need to go home? Not us?"

I study his face carefully, so I see the frown. "Full moon is tonight," he admits. "And I'm not sure if there's enough time to get me to Demonheim, or not, but either way you're best off if I'm far away from you."

I don't even know what makes me do it, can't say it's a conscious thought, but within a moment a vine emerges from the ground and ties our wrists together.

Callum looks down at his new handcuff. "What's this?"

"You'd leave me?" I ask, trying to keep my voice even and failing, hearing the hysteria creep into it. "After what just happened?"

His face looks like I'm tearing him open, and he holds me tighter. "It's not what I want, Marielle. But—"

"But nothing. Don't leave me," I beg. "Do you know—do you know how it felt, to wake up and find you gone?"

It had been like a cord was cut. Like when I was locked inside and mystically chained to the floor, cut off from nature. Being cut off from Callum feels like being cut off from the roots and flowers and trees and grass. It's the same sense of loss inside me, and I won't live with it for a moment longer.

He shudders, and something goes dark behind his eyes. The wolf?

If it is, he shakes it off, but the deep frown doesn't fade. "Marielle, the full moon—"

I use the hand not bound to his to grab the back of his head, pulling him into a bruising kiss.

I pull back, but don't release him, keeping our foreheads still pressed together.

"We still have hours before that," I say.

Chapter Forty-Eight

Callum

Hours.

Damn it, it feels like I'm being torn in two. It's even worse than when I was trying to wrestle control back from the wolf.

I want what Marielle is offering. I want it with my whole soul. I ache for it inside. Her. Me. Tonight, under the full moon.

But I could hurt her, and nothing in the world will let me hurt my mate.

"Marielle, I—"

She kisses me again, hard and demanding, her hand in my hair, guiding me where she wants. Apparently this is her new strategy to shut me up, and I can't exactly say that I don't like it.

"I want this," she says firmly. "I wanted this, you know I did—if we hadn't been interrupted, we both know what we were going to do when we got home."

"The full moon—"

"Believe me, I'm not concerned about the full moon," she interrupts, and a flush covers her face. "I've been—looking forward to it."

Oh?

That feels like a punch to the gut in the best type of way, and it rocks me to my core for a moment before I can process it. "Whatever you want," I manage to say.

What else could I possibly ever say?

Still, some part of me needs to be rational. Some part of me needs to keep it together.

"You'll let me get you ready, before moonrise," I demand, although it probably comes out more like pleading.

She grins, and I register the vine has released my wrist when she reaches her second hand up to hold my head to her. "You think I could wait?"

That snaps the last of my control, the last of my rationality, and I want to lay her in the dirt right there. Maybe we're closer to proper moonrise than I thought, because right then, I can't think past it, can't remember that she deserves better than the ground.

But even the tiny corner of my brain that's rational knows we're not going back to that damn house.

She wiggles in my arms, wanting down, and I can't suppress a growl. She laughs.

"You don't want to do anything right here, trust me," she says, looking at the plants around us, and, well, she'd know more than me. "I know a better spot. If you'll follow me."

Follow her? Anywhere.

I can't tell if that's the wolf or me thinking that, but it doesn't feel like it matters right then. Maybe they've blurred a bit since I turned. Maybe Marielle just brings it out in me.

I let her put her feet on the ground, then grab her hand to show I'll follow wherever she leads me.

She could lead me to a bed of poison ivy, to the edge of a cliff, to the cages under Demonheim—it wouldn't matter. I'm following.

But she leads me to a field of flowers, a riot of colors under the setting sun, and the wolf rumbles happily inside my brain. My mate, in a field of flowers, under the oncoming moon. Was there ever a place more perfect for us?

I don't ask if she's sure again, because I doubt she'd react well. She's sure. And I just have to trust that she'll be honest with me. That she'll tell me to stop, if she needs it.

Until the moon rises, and things become out of my hands.

No. The wolf might be closer to the front, and I might be a little more wild, but the wolf would never hurt her. The wolf loves her, took over my whole body to prove it. It will be fine.

It will be fine. It must be fine.

I force myself not to think about it anymore. I force myself to let it slip to the back of my mind, and bring Marielle, here with me, beautiful and wanting me, to the front.

I pick her up again, hands on her back and thighs, and then lay both of us down on the flowers.

I prop myself up over her, and she looks like a vision there, laid out among the flowers. There's blood in her hair and on her shirt and on her face, although the blood on her face is in weird tracks, and I suddenly remember that the wolf tried to lick her clean. But I ignore all that. She's here in these flowers, she's smiling at me, and that's all that matters.

"Okay?" I ask, just to be sure. Okay, we're here, okay that I'm looming over her, okay that I'm undoubtedly looking at her with more than a little lust in my eyes.

She doesn't answer, just reaches up her arms to wrap them around my neck, pulling me down to her.

It's answer enough, and I let her do it. I move so we're chest to chest, careful to keep most of my weight off of her even as I feel the heat of her against me.

She nuzzles into my neck, and my arms almost collapse under me.

This part isn't new to us, but it feels new now. It feels like a spark, like a building fire, and I feel consumed by it.

I want to be consumed by her, so I reach up to move her from my neck and instead kiss her senseless, deep and bruising, like we can really become one being.

She must be on the same wavelength, because she kisses me back just as hard, gripping at my neck and shoulders, pulling me to her until at last my arms collapse from under me and I can't hold my own weight up anymore.

187

She doesn't seem to notice, even wrapping a leg around my hip, but somewhere in the back of my mind, somehow through this kiss, I worry I might crush her.

I turn us, so I'm on my back and she's on top of me. She pulls back from the kiss, blinking, looking down at me.

It's like a painting, like some grand masterpiece in a museum. Marielle, glowing in the ethereal sunset, red hair a mess and catching the light, lips swollen from our kiss in a wide smile. My breath catches.

Beautiful. Gods, she's the most beautiful thing I've ever seen, and I'm a damn lucky man, and I'm going to make this the best damn thing she's ever felt.

CHAPTER FORTY-NINE

MARIELLE

He seems frozen, watching me, staring at me, and I preen at the attention. I've never been a person who likes attention before, but his eyes make everything inside of me light up and I want more of it.

So I remove my shirt, tossing it somewhere into the field behind us. It's not like I should need it for the rest of the night.

I move to unclip my bra, but Callum is already moving, apparently shaken out of his daze. He sits up under me until I'm straddling his lap. "Gods, Marielle," he groans, reaching for my bra himself.

It falls away, and I frown. "Did you rip it?"

His face turns down, a sheepish expression nevertheless obvious. "I... sorry. Close to the moon. But I'll get a grip on it."

He pulls his hands back between us, and I watch as he wills his claws away. "Good," he says, voice hoarse. "Now I can touch you."

True to his word, his hands come up to cup my breasts, thumbs rubbing at my nipples until they are stiff and peaked. I bite my lip against a moan, but then his hand leaves my breast to stroke over my lower lip.

"Let me hear you," he murmurs. "I want to hear everything tonight."

I nod, and he rewards me by flicking my nipple with the hand still on my breast. "Callum—"

"Yes?" He does it again and I groan, cutting off my train of thought. "What, Marielle?" I can hear his smile without even looking, but when I do look, it's devastating.

That smile. It makes me melt, makes me go soft and wet, and I suddenly want his hands on more than just my breasts.

"Callum, touch me," I plead, rocking my hips against him.

He groans, rocking back. "Gladly. Marielle, I—" but his voice trails off into a deep groan when I rock on him again.

"Pants off," he growls, and there's that almost full-moon voice, the wolf so close to the surface but not breaking through.

I scramble off his lap to get my pants off, then to rip his from him, fingers fumbling as I move. He reaches for me like he wants to pull me back, but then his hands fall as he watches me pull off my clothes.

"You too," I demand, finally getting the damned zipper open. "You too."

He obeys, scrambling, shirt already off before I finish asking the second time, pants following not long after.

I get a split-second to watch him, tall and muscled and oh-so-hard. For me. Backlit by the sunset, out here in nature, looking half-feral with the oncoming moon, he looks magnificent. If you asked me to guess which of us is technically directly descended from gods, I wouldn't pick me.

Now both fully naked, he lunges at me, taking me down to the flowers. He slips both arms around my back, using one to cradle my head as I land.

"Tonight is going to be a lot. So I'm going to make sure you're good and ready for it," he growls, and then his mouth is on my breasts, and his hands down my sides, teasing and stroking.

He moves slower than I expected, teasing and taking his time. I don't know why I expected him to dive right into it, like suddenly having permission to go further would change Callum. Callum has always enjoyed teasing me, winding me up.

Maybe I'm projecting. Maybe I want to go further, faster. I just want to feel him.

I tighten my fingers in his hair, trying to steer him, but he just growls against my breast, then nips lightly at the nipple. I shiver. He's being exceptionally careful, but I feel the brush of his fang, sharper than usual.

Steering him doesn't seem to be working, so, twisting under his hands, I resort to pleading. "Please, Callum, I need—"

His hands find my inner thighs, fingertips brushing feather-light so close to where I want them, and I lose my train of thought with a whimper.

"What do you need, beautiful?" Callum asks, voice a whisper against my dampened nipple, making me shiver. I trail my hands down to his shoulders so I don't accidentally yank on his hair.

"I need you," I grind out, trying once again to push him where I want him to go.

I can feel his smile against my breast. "How do you need me, Marielle?"

Over me, pressing me down, holding me, inside me. All that and more. I need his fingers, his tongue, his cock. I need him pressing me into the flowers beneath us, cementing this bond between us, showing me how good this will always be between us.

But I can't make myself say all that. So I grab his face and haul him up instead of down. He moves easily, eagerly accepting the nearly feral kiss I bestow on him, like I'm the one about to go crazed by the moon.

He responds just as hungrily, sucking at my tongue and letting some of his weight press me into the ground below. I feel every inch of life under the dirt, but I'm much more captivated by the life I feel over me.

Still holding his face in place, I pull away, pressing a few kisses to the corner of his mouth, then his jaw, before I pull back far enough to look him in the eyes. "I want everything you've promised me, Callum," I say as firmly as I can. "Are you going to give it to me?"

The grin I get in return is absolutely feral, sending shivers through me. "Whatever you want, beautiful," he growls, and then he moves down my body.

Chapter Fifty

Callum

I fall on Marielle like her cunt will be my last meal.

There's a time and place for finesse, and I usually possess much more of it. But right now, with the pull of the moon tugging on my senses, with the memory of our recent escape so close behind us, I can't say I possess anything resembling it.

I'm here to feast, to bathe in the taste of my mate, to drown in her juices. Finesse is out the window, all sense of control long gone. This is ritual, hedonistic pleasure, satiating the beast inside me who thinks of nothing, dreams of nothing, but her and her pleasure.

It doesn't seem as if Marielle minds.

She keens loud enough that I'm grateful we're so alone out here, and I grip her hips in both hands, sliding my hands under her glorious ass, raising her cunt closer to my mouth. All the better to eat her with.

She wraps her legs around my head, trapping me exactly where I want to be forever. Her sounds are music to my ears, her nails shifting to her little claws and leaving pleasurable pinpricks on my scalp.

I want her to come on my tongue more than I've ever wanted anything else. Want to taste it, feel it against my face, feel it as her thighs tighten around my head.

The more rational parts of me—whatever's left of them—think that making her come on my tongue will help her relax, will help her get ready, because I will be inside her tonight and I want it to be damn good for her. But most of me, the pieces of me drunk on her cunt, just chase that sweet taste.

She moans my name and grinds against my face as best she can. My hands are too busy holding her to my face to take care of myself, so I'm left to rut against the grass, sparing a brief thought to hope that Marielle used her gifts to thoroughly inspect this field for anything I might not want touching my cock.

She could sit up and inform me right now that every inch of this field was poison ivy and I don't think I'd be able to stop, though, so I rut my hips, imagining what it'll be like rutting into her soon, and circle my tongue over her clit.

She gasps, high and breathy, so I do it again, and again, adding slightly more pressure each time until she's rocking against my face and moaning.

Her claws press into my scalp and her rocking picks up pace, and I know she's close, know I can make her come just like this, make her feel so good and lose control.

A minute later and her thighs tighten around my head, and she gasps my name again and again as her juices flood my tongue, coating every inch of my mouth as I savor her taste.

I can make her come again. I know I can, just like this. I could send her over a second time, already so sensitive and close. It would be easy, and I could keep tasting her—

Marielle makes up my mind for me, pushing at my shoulders until I'm forced to sit back, her legs sliding until her shins are hooked on my shoulders. I sit back on my haunches, watching her.

She's beautiful like this, every inch the debauched angel of nature. No, not an angel—a goddess. She's a goddess, red hair spilling into the flowers, eyes heavy lidded and mouth parted slightly, still red and kiss-swollen, tits heaving with the deep breaths she's still desperately drawing in, cunt wet and puffy and spread beautifully, obscenely open for me to watch.

She removes her legs from my shoulders, letting them fall to the ground. She pulls one back, planting her foot on the ground, leaving her spread wide to my hungry stare.

"Get me ready," she says, the hint of command going right to my already-desperate cock.

"What do you think I was doing?" I ask, smirk in place. I lick my lips just to prove my point, and because I'm already desperate for another taste of her.

She props herself up on her elbows, giving her the ability to look me over, which she does, slowly, eyes clearly lingering on my cock, proud and aching for her.

"That," she says, almost delicately, "is going to take some effort to get inside me. And you promised to be inside me tonight."

I did promise. And I'm thinking a little clearer than I was a moment ago, so I can acknowledge that I'd really like to be inside her at least once before the moon's pull takes hold of me.

"You want my fingers inside you, beautiful?" she nods. "Then lie back, let me get you ready."

She scrambles to obey, and her tits shake as she practically collapses back to the ground. I watch them bounce for a moment, distracted by how spell-binding they are, how I want them in my mouth again. But then she spreads her legs even further open, and my attention is diverted.

Her red curls are soaked from her last orgasm, her cunt wet and open. It's a little puffy already, and I shiver as I imagine what she'll look like in the morning.

Glorious, beautiful, some sort of sex goddess out here in her field of wildflowers—

"Callum?"

"You are so beautiful," I rasp out, and I don't wait anymore. I check my hand, making sure my claws are away, willing the wolf to understand they need to stay that way.

One finger slides in easily, not an inch of resistance left there. So I follow it with a second finger, basking in her little gasp when I crook them just so.

I do it again, and again, listening to that gasp get louder, more desperate, and then I back off, spreading my fingers, teasing at her walls, getting her ready for me.

I could make her come like this. I could make her squeeze around my fingers. And I almost do, but Marielle grabs my wrist to stop me.

My eyes snap to her face. "What is it? Something wrong?" Does she want to stop?

"I want you inside me," she tells me, voice breathy. "I want... gods, Callum. Now."

I don't ask if she's sure. I've done enough of that and she's done enough to make her feelings on the matter well known. And she's asking for what she wants—demanding it, really—which is everything I've wanted for us since the day I met her.

I carefully withdraw my fingers, watching her cunt briefly gape as I pull them out, watching a trail of slick between my fingers and her opening. Then I take my slick-covered hand and stroke my fingers over my too-long neglected cock, rubbing her wetness onto me.

The last drags of the sunset cast her skin with an ethereal glow, and I can't help myself. I fall forward, hovering over her, braced on one forearm, the other hand still on my cock. I seek her lips for a kiss, which she gives me.

"This okay?" I ask, pulling back just far enough to ask. "Like this?"

She grabs at my shoulders and locks her left leg around my hip, nodding before she seeks another kiss, which I eagerly give her.

There's only one way to be physically more connected to her than I am right now, and I want it desperately. Her foot digs into the back of my thigh, nudging me forward, and I don't need any more prompting.

I go slow, breaking the kiss so I can watch her face the entire time, watching for any signs of discomfort as I push inside of her.

Wolves aren't small, I'm not small, but Marielle is, and the last thing I want to do is hurt her.

But evidently I prepared her well, because her legs fall open even wider with a shaky little gasp, her claws digging into my shoulders, and I rock into her, slowly, inch by inch.

It's the best kind of torture. Tight and hot, her warm cunt pulling me, coaxing me deeper into her. I have to fight to keep my eyes open, and all I can think is that, now that I've felt this, I never want to leave.

At last, I'm inside her entirely, swallowed up by her, and it's like I was always meant to be here. Like I was born to be inside her.

"Good?" I check, pressing kisses along her jaw and neck, wanting to give her a moment to adjust.

She doesn't answer for a long moment, but then she rolls her hips onto me, as if testing it. "Good."

She rolls her hips again, a little more sure this time, and I can't suppress my growl. "Good," I repeat, and I pull out before rocking back into her.

She lets out a little cry, and I do it again until that cry shifts into a long moan. "That's it, beautiful," I murmur, reaching down between us to find her clit, giving it a light stroke, making her arch her back. "That's it. Good?"

She nods frantically and tries to push closer to me, tries to rock herself against me. I don't change my pace, keeping it even and deep, wanting to build this up for her, wanting it to be so good that she sees stars.

I bend to nip at her breasts, then suck one nipple into my mouth, laving it with my tongue. She moans, and every instinct in me tells me to bite. That I'm satisfying my mate, that I'm driving her wild, making her feel good. That I'm doing what I'm meant for, and now I need to seal it, put my mark on her.

Not. Yet. The moon isn't even fully visible yet, and I will not let anything interfere with her first time.

Her hands go to my hair, tugging and pushing, begging for more. "Callum, Callum, oh gods, please—"

I raise my face. "Please what, beautiful? You know I'll give you anything." To emphasize this, I stroke over her clit again, applying just a little more pressure.

She gasps and bucks against my hand, and her cunt squeezes around me, desperately pulling me in deeper.

Gods, she wants to come. Needs it, more like. It's written clear as day across her face, in every movement of her body against mine, in the way her claws pull at me, like she's going to physically tug me into her, consume me.

And I'm here to give my mate anything and everything she wants.

I keep my fingers on her clit and return my mouth to her nipple, sucking and flicking with my tongue, waiting, knowing it won't be long, that she's already close.

Her nails dig in to the point of near-pain—the most welcome pain of my damn immortal life—and I feel her walls squeezing around me. I release her breast to watch her face instead, wanting to watch her fall apart with my cock inside her, knowing full well it will drag me over as well.

Her back bows off the ground, her head thrown back. Her eyes are squeezed shut and I watch as her mouth falls open in a wordless cry.

Ravishing, beautiful, divine beyond anything I've ever known or imagined—

Gods, she's so tight, and I'm losing control. I pump into her welcoming cunt once, twice more, and then my orgasm sweeps through me. My hips stutter and I bellow her name for the world to hear.

Her claws, dug so deep in me during her own orgasm, release me, her small hands gently petting my neck and shoulders now. My hips twitch half-heartedly a few times, but I reluctantly pull out so I can roll onto my back, pulling her on top of me.

She uses a hand on my chest to push herself up slightly, watching me. Her hair is a tangled—still bloody—mess, but her eyes and skin glow, and I preen a bit. I did that. I gave Marielle that.

I want to say something, to do something besides stare at her, but I can't. They say a first time with your mate is world-shaking, and I have to agree. Marielle just re-aligned my world.

She shifts so she can kiss me, and this at least I can do. The kiss is slow, lazy almost, and she pulls away after a moment to kiss my cheek, my jaw, my chin. "Thank you," she whispers. "I never... thank you."

"Thank you," I respond, trying to redirect her to kiss her mouth again, to have that with her. She gives in easily, kissing me long and slow. My hands find her waist, holding her to me, and I feel her move so she's straddling me.

And then I feel it.

Moonrise.

CHAPTER FIFTY-ONE

MARIELLE

I can feel it the moment he changes.

It's nothing so obvious as his appearance, although I can feel the scrape of his longer fangs too.

It's the way his grip on my waist tightens, the way his kiss becomes more aggressive and demanding.

Moonrise.

Deep down, as much as I wanted this, as I planned on us being together under the moon tonight, I thought the first hints of this change would scare me. That it would be overwhelming, that it would feel that I was losing Callum to this change, even if I didn't want it to. That my soft, gentle, kind mate is being swallowed and I would be left to... well, to the wolves.

But that's not how I feel at all. It's not fear I feel, nor anxiety or anything even close. It's exhilaration, I think. Eager anticipation, knowing what's coming. I welcome it.

It's like the moon has a pull on me, too.

Callum breaks the kiss, licking at my neck, and groans. "Marielle."

I pull back so I can see him, can look him in the eyes. He's there. I see him watching me. The same man, the same mate who I just made love to for the first time, the same man who I love. But something flickers behind his eyes, and I think it's the same wolf I saw in the cell.

He sniffs suddenly, and I know Callum has a sense of smell that far exceeds mine, but he's usually not so obvious about scenting like this.

In a move so fast I can barely track it, Callum is on his feet and I'm in his arms. I gasp and grab at him, looking for purchase, but of course his arms hold me tight. He'd never let me fall.

He sniffs again. The first time, I thought he was scenting me. Scenting us, the combined leaking mess between my thighs, the way our bare skin has touched and rubbed and combined now. But he tilts his head, looking for something, and sniffs again.

Seeming to determine a direction, he starts moving.

All our clothes are still in the field, but that's the least of my concerns. I wrap my arms tightly around his neck. "Where're you taking me?"

He stops moving entirely, nuzzling against my hair, my neck. "Take... care..." he bites out, like words are difficult, distant from him. For all I know, they are. Words probably aren't a priority for the wolf.

Of course, I thought making love again and again and again would be the wolf's biggest priority, but apparently Callum has something else in mind.

I don't protest. Callum's never hurt me, never steered me wrong. And I'm not scared of him, no matter how much control the wolf does or doesn't have.

Callum has found a stream, about a half a mile back in the woods. I raise an eyebrow at him. "Aren't we just going to get dirty again?"

I hope we are. I'd been promised that full moons were a night of endless pleasure and debauchery. And it turns out, with Callum, I'm very much enjoying the debauchery.

He makes me feel things I didn't even know I could feel. He has since the very first time I asked him to put his hands and mouth on me, so I didn't expect any difference now. But it was transcendent. Not a lick of pain, just pleasure, building and building and building, carefully stoked by him until it spilled over spectacularly. And I want more.

I'm apparently going to have to wait, because Callum walks us into the stream, not stopping until the water is past his waist. I laugh, clinging to him tighter, trying to keep out of the undoubtedly chilly water. "Callum! What is this?"

Apparently me wanting to keeping myself out of the water doesn't appeal to the wolf, because Callum sets me on my feet. I go up on my tip-toes against the cool water, and Callum uses one arm to clasp me tightly to him, although even as high as the water is, I doubt the current is strong enough to truly knock me off my feet.

Then he cups water in his free hand and lets it fall over my hair. I shiver, but suddenly understand.

Take care, the wolf had said. He's taking care of me.

Bathing me, because, I realize as I see the water running off me, there's been blood on me.

I give him a moment to get me clean—at least until it seems like the water is running clear—and turn in his arms. "Can I bathe you too?"

He spreads the arm not still holding me, as if inviting me. As if saying I'm yours.

He's not covered in blood, so I take this as an opportunity to touch, to trail my fingers over his arms, up his biceps to his shoulders, to his chest and down to his stomach, tightly corded with muscles and seemingly held tighter under my touch. Like he's holding his breath.

I run my hand further down. But just when my hand breaks the water, something inside Callum seems to snap. He grabs me up, using his enormous hands on my hips, on my backside, to haul me up, encouraging me to wrap my legs around his waist.

He was being remarkably patient, considering everything I'd been told about the full moon. But that's seemingly over, and I laugh, grabbing him around the neck, trying to pull him into a kiss.

He growls, low and rumbly and much, much closer to the wolf inside him than I've heard any other time. Then he tilts his head into my kiss, hefting me tighter in his grip, his fingers pressing into my skin. I rock forward towards him, hoping to encourage him further.

I can feel it building between my thighs again. I'm soft and wet and wanting there again, and it wouldn't take much for him to slide into me. My muscles clench around nothing at just the thought.

Movement jars me and I break the kiss to realize he's walking us out of the stream. He growls again, tilting his head forward, looking for my kiss, and I eagerly give it to him.

He goes to his knees on the bank, then lays me down on the ground, following me so our kiss never breaks. I release my hold on him, letting my hands sink into the dirt, feeling the earth around us. Half of me is just looking to ground myself, his kiss already driving me higher, making me needy. Half of me is trying to feel out what grows around us, still conscious enough to know I don't want certain plants touching my exposed naked skin.

But it's safe enough. My fingertips sharpen once again to claws, control seemingly completely gone from me, and sink into the earth. It's like the energy there feeds me, like when I take the life force from plants to heal. Except I don't need to heal.

I feel over-energized. I feel like I could take on the world. I feel it thrumming in my veins, not unlike the power I'd summoned in that basement.

I feel alive in a way I never have before, every nerve ending thrumming, so damn alive. With some effort, I make myself release my hold on the earth below me, force myself to focus enough to retract my claws so I can reach for Callum again. But it changes nothing; the energy from the earth beneath me is still pumping through me.

"Callum," I breathe, feeling high on this, whatever this is. Him, me, us, the earth, the moon—I couldn't begin to guess. Maybe it's all of them. "Callum, I need you inside me again."

I know words are difficult for him like this, but his growl and nip at my collarbone tells me he agrees. I spread my thighs as wide as I can, shifting so he can kneel between them.

He moves his mouth from my skin and sits back on his heels, and the hunger my mate looks at me with sends my own hunger spiraling higher. I need him. Now.

He puts his hands on my hips, rubbing the skin there for just a moment before he lifts, positioning me so he can easily slide inside me.

He pushes in faster this time, and my eyes roll back in my head, my hands once again curling into claws in the dirt. We did this less than an hour ago, and yet it feels like he's stretching me wider than I've ever been stretched all over again. Opening me, touching me in ways that I ache for, that only he can reach, that only he can satisfy.

My body has been a mystery to me, territory well explored, but never by me. But now here we are, and Callum seems to already know every inch of me, and is taking me along for the ride.

I grasp at his shoulders, trying not to grip him too hard and likely failing. I can't help it, needing to hold him, to pull him to me, like I can keep him inside me forever, push him deeper, merge into one being.

"Callum," I whine, legs circling around his hips, head falling back under his feverish pace. "Callum."

"Mate," he growls against my breast, teeth scraping the flesh as he makes his way to wrap his lips around my nipple, sucking hard enough for me to see stars. He thrusts harder, and I moan, throaty and needy, trying to convey how good he feels, how desperate for more I am—

He must understand, releasing an approving growl against my skin. We don't have much need for words, apparently.

Good. I can barely think, can barely focus on anything that's not his shaft inside me, impossibly big and filling every inch of me. Or his lips on my skin, having abandoned my breast to trail up to my neck, to my jaw, to my ears, sucking and scraping his teeth as he goes. He nips lightly at the pointed tip, teasing, and I groan as I arch up into him.

My hands fall from his shoulders, landing beside me, claws completely out of my control and sinking into the dirt, connecting me back to the earth. It becomes a feedback cycle, energy and pleasure pouring in from every direction until I'm alight with it, every nerve on fire as he touches me.

He nips my other ear now, and I force my eyes open to see him above me. I want to see his face, want to hold his eyes and hope he can see in mine what he does to me—

The moon peeks over the tree line, bright and full and just behind Callum's head, and it feels like an extra jolt of energy through me.

Beautiful. I haven't seen a full moon in two hundred years.

And every month, I get it just like this. Full and glorious and making Callum, sweat-slicked and passionate and frenzied, glow underneath her light.

"Callum," I make myself say. I want him to look at me, want him to kiss me, want to have him right here, with me, completely with me. Because he's going to make me come, I can feel it.

He doesn't move, kissing my ear again, then my jaw, slow presses of his lips at odds with his furiously pounding hips.

I force my hands from the earth to grab at his hair, tugging him where I want him. That tiny bit of force seems to be enough, and he moves easily in my hold.

I kiss him and he eagerly returns it, deep and sloppy. Wild.

Wolfish.

When I pull away to breathe, I keep my hands in his hair, keep him where I want him. Then I press kisses to the corner of his mouth, his jaw, down his neck.

This man, this raw, powerful man who is filling me so good, so completely, who's making me feel things I didn't know a person could feel—he's mine. He's mine, my mate, mine forever. And I'll see the full moon again next month, and every month thereafter, just like this.

My mate.

The possessive thought loops in my head, not releasing me as I grab Callum a little tighter, let my heels dig into the backs of his thighs. I kiss his neck once more, and then, possessiveness completely taking me over, bite.

Callum goes completely still in my grip for a second, then pounds against me fast and uncoordinated for a brief moment, rhythm completely lost. He bellows a wordless cry, loud enough to make the trees around us shake, and fills me with his come.

I release his neck from my teeth and then freeze. What just happened? What did I do?

He growls again, this time low and possessive and, I think, pleased. More like a cat purring, maybe.

Then he moves to kiss me senseless.

I cry out when he slips out of me, breaking the kiss. I'm throbbing, so close to what I needed, and now I'm empty, my body leaking his come as my walls throb internally. I want to cry, I want something, I need—

Callum doesn't disappoint. Without breaking our kiss, he rolls us onto our sides, then rolls onto his back, finally breaking our lips apart. I take a second to look him over, seeing the intensity in his eyes, the way they bore into me.

I see the bite mark on his neck, too. I didn't break skin, but he'll have a bruise for however long it lasts before his healing takes care of it. Something primal, something I didn't even know was in me, sparks with satisfaction.

His hands find my hips and haul me over him. I thought he meant for me to ride him, but he's not ready to enter me again yet, although I have no doubt he will be soon. Instead, he lifts me like I weigh nothing to him, sitting me right on his face.

I squeak, having the presence of mind to worry about my weight against his face, of cutting off his oxygen. He growls, the vibrations making me moan and temporarily forget my attempt to get off of him. Then his hands clamp on my hips, pulling me back down to his mouth.

"Callum, I—"

He doesn't let me finish, just starts licking between my thighs, making me gasp and involuntarily tighten my legs around his head.

Oh, gods, he—

I've been feeling our mingled fluids leaking out of me, down my thighs, since he pulled out of me, and now here Callum is, his face buried there, licking me like I'm delicious, like he's desperate for me. I can barely breathe, each breath a chore as he sends me higher and higher, and I start rocking against his face, concerns about crushing him apparently forgotten.

"Callum, please," I plead, with absolutely no idea what I'm asking for, other than the fact that I need to come, need it more than I ever have before, that every touch of his tongue, every time he drives it into me like he's starving for me, is pushing me to places I didn't know were possible.

His fingers squeeze my thighs, as if he can crush me any closer to his face, and he sets in even more intently, driving inside me with his tongue.

He groans against me, the vibrations making me clench and I lose control. I buck against his face as my orgasm washes through me, gasping his name and riding his tongue as I shatter apart.

This is transcendent, this is the pleasure I never could have imagined, this is—

I gasp as I come back to myself, and realize belatedly I must be crushing him, suffocating him. I try to release the grip my thighs have on his head, try to lift my weight, but Callum just growls against me and uses his big hands to hold my thighs in place.

I reach a shaking hand down to stroke his hair. "Callum, I need to move."

He growls again, and then, to really send the message, sucks my over sensitized clit between his lips, making me gasp and buck against his face.

"O-oh, gods, Callum," I gasp, unable to stop my hips from thrusting shallowly, begging for more. "N-no, I want—" He sucks again, temporarily deviating my train of thought. "I want you inside me again, Callum." He sucks again, lost in the taste of me, but I suddenly know what to do. I tighten my grip on his hair and make my voice as firm as I possibly can. "Mate. I need to be filled by you."

That makes him freeze beneath me, entirely still, and, faster than I can track, I'm on my hands and knees with Callum behind me, spreading my thighs a little wider, using one hand to pet over my back while he lines himself up with the other.

I'm so wet and open that the tip slides in easily, and as soon as I feel that slight stretch, I push back the rest of the way, moaning as he fills me entirely. I start rocking against him, gasping as he presses so deep inside me, wanting, needing, more.

He growls and puts both hands on my hips, stopping my movements. I get ready to complain, but he rocks into me hard, using his hands to pull me back onto him, and I see stars.

I'm not going to last long like this. His movements are sure and strong, touching every inch inside me, making me feel him, and even with recently coming on his tongue, I'm still on the edge.

I dig my claws into the ground to anchor myself and let his name spill past my lips in a constant, steady moan. *Callum Callum Callum Callum—*

He growls again and leans forward, pressing his weight along my back. Then his lips find my skin, sucking the tip of my ear, making my eyes roll back into my head.

His lips make their way to my neck, pressing a series of kisses there before his thrusts speed up. He's close, and so am I.

His teeth latch onto my skin, and there's a brief pain, but then it feels like sparks, like his bite has somehow electrified me even further, and I'm coming.

It rushes through my whole body, not an inch of me left untouched by this orgasm. I have enough presence of mind to realize that Callum is also coming, that he's released his teeth from my neck to frantically kiss and lick at the spot as we both ride the pleasure.

My arms fail to support my weight, and I collapse forward. But Callum catches me around the middle, sliding out of me as he uses his strength to move me so I'm lying on my back, and he's hovering over me once more.

I whine, squirming slightly at the empty feeling, at the feeling of wetness spilling out of me and down my thighs. I feel wrecked, messy.

And the way Callum hungrily looks down at me, I feel like it's an achievement. I smile up at him, and I know we're nowhere near done for the night.

CHAPTER FIFTY-TWO

CALLUM

When the hold of the moon releases me, I have my head pillowed on Marielle's beautiful tits and her hand stroking through my hair.

It takes a moment for every part of last night to come back to me, like it's a dream I'm remembering. I was aware of every moment, just distantly. Like I was not entirely in control, maybe.

But then I remember it all. Remember how she felt, how she tasted, how she moved...

It's a testament to exactly how long we fucked under the full moon that even the memories in every explicit, beautiful detail can't quite make me hard again.

"You back with me?" she asks softly, her hands still making slow, lazy paths through my hair.

"I'm here," I promise her, not willing to move my head from its current resting place. "Was everything good for you?" I check.

I remember everything, I think, and she seemed to enjoy it. But under the moon, I'm not in full possession of my rationality. What if the wolf had pushed her? Would I have been able to tell?

"Everything was wonderful," she sighs, voice low and happy. "I feel..."

Sore, I imagine. Sore and probably filthy. But judging by her voice, also very good, and I want to preen a bit at that.

I made my mate feel that way. I gave her pleasure, made the full moon an enjoyable experience for her. Made sex something she sounds like she enjoys. I gave that to her.

And now I have eternity to keep giving it to her. Was there ever a luckier male?

Her breasts are soft and warm under my face, but I want to see her, want to start thinking about the day, so I reluctantly force myself up.

The first thing I notice is the riot of wildflowers around us, and I blink, scanning my memories. I know the wolf had a single-minded focus last night, but I can't imagine I missed all of that.

Marielle must notice my gaze. "They were there when I woke up," she says, voice still quiet. "I'm not sure..."

But I am. I'm so sure that I made my mate feel so good that she couldn't help it. That my powerful druidic mate connected with the earth, pouring pleasure and power into it, and this is the result.

I know I'm grinning, and I know it probably looks stupid, but I can't help it.

She shoves lightly at my shoulder. "Stop it."

"Why?" I ask, catching the hand she shoved at me with to lift it to my lips, kissing her fingertips. "Look how powerful my mate is. Look how happy you are."

Happy and well-pleased. She made the very earth reflect her feelings, and I preen.

She huffs, but concedes. "I am. Happy, that is. Are you?"

I look away from the flowers to focus entirely on her. "I am the happiest wolf in the world," I tell her seriously. "I am the luckiest wolf, too, and I... I..." I don't have words, so I growl a bit and lean down to kiss her neck, finding where I put the bite mark from last night. "Mate," I mumble against her. "I am so lucky to have such a perfect mate."

She sighs. "We should call Chase."

I growl, unable to help it, thinking of anyone else near her when we're still so close to the moon, to our first mating. I bury the growl in her neck, but I know she hears it. "I'm sure they're still asleep."

"The last your family heard, we were both kidnapped," she reminds me, annoyingly rational. "We should tell them we're fine." She shifts under me. "Besides. I want a bath, and not in a creek."

A bath. I can get her a bath. Right. I reluctantly lift my head from her neck, determined to take care of her properly.

A hot meal, a long bath, and maybe by then I'd be up for taking care of her again. I'm suddenly becoming more and more understanding of Bryce's three-year honeymoon.

"Chase Crae," I call.

Marielle groans. "I didn't mean—our clothes, Callum."

Right. It's too late now, though, because Chase is already appearing and looking decidedly unimpressed with us.

I use my body to cover Marielle's naked form and turn to glare at Chase, but he already has a much more piercing stare leveled.

"Do you two have any idea how fucking worried we've been?" he snaps. Then, completely heedless of our nudity and my growling, he marches forward, gets a hand on each of us, and disappears.

***

Chase is apparently in a mood to be merciless, because we reappear in Celia's study, completely full of the entire family, and still completely naked.

And on top of that, the bastard takes his energy payment from me, so I nearly fall on my ass as soon as we land.

I get my bearings and try to use my body to block Marielle. I'm sure every poor soul here has seen me naked more than once, but Marielle wouldn't want them to see her naked.

And honestly, hours after sealing our mating bond? I'm not sure how well I'd deal with it, either.

Heath recovers first, tossing me the throw blanket from the back of the old leather armchair, which I take gratefully, turning to give it to Marielle, helping her wrap it around herself.

"Gods," Celia mutters, rubbing the bridge of her nose, but she throws me a sweatshirt and I use it to cover myself, maneuvering the two of us to the armchair, pulling Marielle onto my lap.

"Glad to see you both survived," Mae says, breaking the stand-off first.

Marielle squirms in my lap. "Sorry, I—I know I should have found a way to contact you all, but by the time we got free, the moon was practically risen and we just..." I can see the flush creeping up her ears. Apparently Marielle can moan for me under the moon for hours, can guide me around by my hair and steer me where she wants with her bite, but she still can't talk about it. Adorable.

I can't resist. I lean forward to nuzzle at that reddening ear, making her shiver in my hold.

The room is absolutely dead silent, and I reluctantly pull away from Marielle long enough to look around. I'm met with steely gazes and tense expressions, and I decide I don't want to know how their full moon went.

"Remind us to buy you a phone, Marielle," Mae eventually says.

"They would have taken it from me."

"How'd you get away?" Bryce asks.

That I can answer. "She killed them all," I inform the room. My brave, fearless, strong mate, who made the plants and the very earth give her what she needed, who saved us both.

Chase whistles reluctantly. "Badass."

"Not all of them," Marielle protests. "Callum helped."

She took out most of them, though.

"And I definitely couldn't have done it without whatever you gave me," she adds, looking at Mae.

Mae frowns. "That should've given you a few hours on your feet. Maybe helped you focus. Not allowed you to hulk out or anything."

"Well, it made me stronger," she insists.

"No, Marielle," I tell her. "I think that was all you."

I don't want to debate it with her right now. I want to wait until we're alone, until we have a bit of privacy. And then I want to tell her I want her to start training with those gifts more, in addition to the knives. I want to see what she can do.

And I want her to have a choice in what comes next. Because if she does choose to come into battle with me, I need to know she's ready.

Celia, the consummate warrior queen, seems to be on the same wavelength as me. "Update on your attackers," she demands.

"Same group who held Marielle before."

"We killed every last one at their original base," Heath says. "I made sure of it."

I'm sure he did. And after he saw Marielle and realized she was my mate, I'm sure he made it slow, too. But that doesn't change anything. "There were more."

"Do you think there are still more?" Celia asks.

"Yes." It's Marielle who answers, voice confident, and only I can feel the way she tenses saying it. "What they're doing, what they did, there are more of them."

Celia doesn't question her conclusion, which I appreciate. I would have said the same thing, but it's good to know that they take Marielle's word the same way they would mine. "Then it's our job to go after them," she says, steepling her fingers in front of her, and I can already see the wheels turning in her head. "They're a danger to the entire world, with what they do. An abomination. Not to mention, they went after two of our own. And we can't let that go."

Bethany lays a hand on Celia's shoulder, squeezing. Trying to keep her calm, I know, and I hate that I have to ruin the effort. "When they had me, I'd turned," I admit, and ignore the sharp intakes of breath. "When they went after Marielle like that. And I remember... Marielle, do I remember right? They said that with the full moon, they could've used me. In the way they used to use you." That my inferior ingredients would have been possible to use.

She nods shakily. "You remember right."

Celia's eyes go dark. "Then it's urgent, then. They're a threat to all of us. Heath, Chase, I want to know everything there is to know. Everything else gets bumped down the list. Bryce—we need everyone we know to be prepared for this. And Callum..." Her eyes shift to me, boring into me, and I sit up a little straighter. I can't help it; Celia is my sister, and she rarely pulls rank. But she's also my queen. "Get ready to go to war."

I nod, wrapping my arms around Marielle even tighter.

We're not going to get that three-year honeymoon after all.

***

Bethany is the good sport who offers to go get us actual clothes so we don't need to do the walk of shame back to our house like this. As soon as she's gone, and Celia's focus has become less intense, Chase cracks a lascivious grin. "Really trying to get me to lose the bet, huh, Callum?"

Heath elbows him, but it's too late. "What bet?" Marielle asks.

The room goes silent, and I know every bastard here is leaving this to me. "After you first came here, there was, uh, a bet going around. A lot of the wolves apparently got into it." I flush, thinking about some of the conversations I'd overheard. "When Celia first mated Bethany, we knew there wasn't going to be a typical direct line for an heir, so we all decided that, whoever the first-born of the four of us was, that would be the heir. There's a bit of a bet if the baby will be ours, or Bryce and Mae's."

"Oh," she mumbles, head ducking down, and I can't have that.

I squeeze her lightly and lay a kiss on her neck, right over where I bit her last night. "No one's taking it too seriously. No one's worried about an heir—we're pretty much immortal and there's four of us, anyways. You get to decide when you want to have a kid."

"Damn right," Mae says, and I see her squeezing Bryce's hand as she speaks. "We've got time and I want some just for us first. I'm doing everything I can to prevent pregnancy."

Marielle nods slowly, as if absorbing this. "There are herbs for that," she murmurs.

"Yeah, like a NuvaRing."

"Not an herb but that too." She looks sideways at Chase. "What's the bet?"

Chase grins at her. "So much money. So hold out a bit for me, alright?"

Marielle snorts. "We'll see."

I think she just says it to fuck with him. I think she does want to wait, and I wouldn't be surprised if she has some ancient herbal thing soon. I make a mental note to ask Mae to talk her through modern birth control and anything she might not yet know. Just so the decision is one hundred percent Marielle's.

But someday, would the baby have her red hair? Her pointed little ears? Would they be more wolf or more druid?

Someday, I'm fully confident we'll find out.

But until then, I have a fight to plan, and a mate to spend every spare second worshiping, and I can think of no better thing to be doing.

CHAPTER FIFTY-THREE

MARIELLE

After we get dressed in the clothes Bethany brings us, we go back to our house. I know there will be more meetings. Serious ones, too. Because the wolves are going to war.

Callum holds my hand as we walk. He barely stopped touching me to pull on pants earlier. And honestly, even without some instinct compelling me, I feel like I don't want to let him go either. Like every second I'm not touching him, I might lose him entirely.

"I don't want you going without me," I tell him as soon as we shut the door to our home. It might just be my imagination, but I feel like we both relax, with us on one side of the door and the world on the other. "To wherever this war takes you," I clarify.

"It won't be a war," he corrects almost automatically, checking the door lock before steering me towards the couch. "Proper immortal wars are all but a thing of the past."

"So what would you call it?"

He considers. "A targeted strike. And it's for a good cause."

I swallow. "I know." And I do. I should feel something more than a burning righteousness maybe, but I don't. These people hurt me, hurt Callum. Hurt Theo. Hurt others.

They sell spells for enslavement, turning other's minds against them. And who's to say I'm the only halfling they cut to pieces? For all I know, they might have locations all over the world, cutting organs out of a hundred halflings they've captured.

"It is a good cause," I continue. "And I'm coming with you."

"I know," is all he says, and then slides his arms under me so he can seat me across his lap. "I want to do some training first. You're good with knives, and I think we can introduce you to a few other weapons too. And your magic... I know I don't know many druids, Marielle, but I bet few of them are as powerful as you. It's that halfling power, I bet. I want you to practice with it. Because it's deadly, but I can't have you passing out every time."

I want to point out that I'd been knocked unconscious, been terrified, been teleported against my will, and was regrowing an eye that I'd just removed myself, but I don't say it. He's not wrong, and we don't know what type of situations we'll find ourselves in.

"Plus," he admits lowly, running his nose up my neck, "I highly doubt I could leave you here without going insane."

I don't feel too differently, honestly. "Deal. Training starts tomorrow morning."

He growls playfully and squeezes around my middle. "My mate is a strict task-master, huh? Couldn't even give us a fully uninterrupted day first?"

But I won't be swayed. "The sooner we're ready to face this, the sooner we take care of it the sooner we can start the rest of forever."

"Forever," he says against my neck, then pulls back to grin. "I like the sound of that. And when we start that forever, we're going to take a honeymoon so long, it makes Bryce and Mae seem tame in comparison."

I like how that sounds too. I move so I'm straddling his lap, and wrap my arms around his neck, my fingers sliding into his hair. He looks up at me, mouth parted slightly, hands slowly traveling to hold my waist. "But in the meantime, we have the rest of the day," I invite.

His hands immediately travel to my thighs, fingers digging in as he hoists me up when he stands. I laugh and wrap my legs around him, holding tight as he begins moving to the bedroom upstairs. "Don't have to tell me twice," he mutters, already looking for my mouth for a kiss that I happily return.

LOOKING FOR MORE?

Subscribe to my newsletter for an exclusive bonus scene about Callum and Marielle, and be the first to know about new books! Sign up at addyjameswrit er.com.

WHAT TO READ NEXT?

Loving the Crae family and looking for more fated mates, found family, and supernatural tension? Check out Bryce and Mae's story!

Bryce contains tropes such as: grumpy wolf shifter, fated mates, she doesn't think she's good enough (he thinks she's the best), and sassy witch.

***

Bryce

"You've got to be kidding me," I say, looking bleakly at my sister across her desk.

The look she returns is decidedly unimpressed. Good: Two can play at that game. And while all four of us Crae siblings might be able to be grumpy bastards, I've always taken the cake on that score. So I know I can hold out longer than her.

She knows it too. We've only been having these staring contests for a thousand years now. Sometimes I think we were having them in the cradle.

"I've been with the humans all week," I try, but the set of her eyebrows tells me she's not cutting me any slack.

It's true, too, and that's the worst of it. I've spent a week dealing with human politics and that always leaves me drained. Humans really are tiring, but when politicians get it into their mind to try to pass a law that would allow logging on the mountains that help hide our home, someone has to play the environmental lobbyist and go grease the right palms. And that someone is always me.

I want a meal, a full night's sleep, and some time where I have to talk to absolutely no one if I don't want to. I do not want to get on a plane to anywhere, much less to New York.

New York stinks, and the steel and concrete always makes me feel claustrophobic. And, more to the point, it's not home.

"Look," Celia says, tapping the fingers of her left hand on the desk. "I know you're tired, I get it. But she's been doing the border enchantment for us for a hundred and ten years and I can't get ahold of her."

"Send someone else," I say, just barely avoiding snarling at my sister. My queen, who is usually pretty tolerant of our bullshit, but might just snap back if I'm too much of an asshole. "Send Callum." Border enchantments sound more like his business than mine.

She rolls her eyes. "I'm not sending Callum away when our border enchantment is weaker than it's been in a century."

"Chase." He could get there and back in an hour, and I could go the fuck to bed.

She actually grimaces. "Chase and Heath just got back from an assignment for me."

"So did I."

"Chase took a shot to the neck. He's fine, but you do not want to get between those two right now. Trust me."

So she'd considered asking them, at least. And now I'm the only option left to her.

Anyone could get on a plane to New York. Anyone could march into the shop and demand our border enchantment. But the question is, do we want just anyone doing that?

No. Celia wants one of us, and it's going to be me. I'm the best, and I always represent our pack when we need the best. When we need the job done and done right, I'm Celia's go-to. Always have been.

She pushes a paper with an address across the table at me. "Plane tickets have already been purchased," she says, sliding the printed ticket across next.

I glower at it. Economy. With a layover.

"Bethany's been cooking?" she offers when I look up.

It's not the worst consolation prize I've ever gotten.

***

I barely have time to savor my meal before I'm off to my house to re-pack a bag so I can get to the airport on time.

My house looks like someone hasn't been living here for ages. Not that I do too much with it when I am here, truth be told. But the lack of use is showing, and I have to hastily wipe dust off the countertop as I dig through the drawer for a human ID that matches the name Celia used on my plane ticket.

The whole point of our village is to be out of the way of humans, so it's quite a drive to get to the airport, leaving me just enough time to get through the infuriating process of airport security and barely make it to the plane before the doors close.

I swing my bag into the overhead compartment and then go to sit down. It's a middle seat. Of course.

How else did I expect this day to go?

I'm too big to fly economy, never mind in a damn middle seat. And the humans might not know what I am, but something always sets them on edge around me. They always know, deep down, that we're not like them. And now I'm shoved between two of them.

I close my eyes. It's going to be a long flight.

***

After a connection where I barely have time to eat a meal, another middle seat, and helping three old ladies with their overhead bags, I'm left standing in the middle of the busy terminal at JFK.

Humans really are a drain on my patience.

I get a cab outside the airport, not quite having enough energy to handle a subway today. The smells in those places are always nearly overwhelming for the wolf in me, and there are too many humans who might inadvertently touch me. So a cab it is.

I give him the address on Canal Street and settle in for the ride, hoping I can get this over with. That whatever witch has been ducking Celia's calls will be easy to convince to come back to work, and that I can get back on the plane tonight.

Not that I really want to fly again so soon, but if it's my own bed at the end of it and not another hotel, I'm all for it.

I smell the shop before I see it, the scent masking even the garbage and piss smell of New York. Magic, and a particularly strong reek of it. I wrinkle my nose and brace myself for what's up ahead.

***

Mae

I have my alarm set loud enough to wake the dead.

It actually doesn't sound too dissimilar to the bell my great-uncle, who claims he's a necromancer, uses in his rituals. And it has only marginally better luck waking me than it does corpses.

After a minute of scrambling, I turn the alarm off, then force myself to roll out of bed. Coffee is already brewing, and I go through the motions of getting dressed while it finishes.

When it's done, I stumble over to it, dumping in one of the vials I keep in a line next to the coffeepot. In lieu of any cream or sugar, this little bottle will do nicely.

222

I suck it down, still piping hot. Proper witch's brew, there it is. With enough kick to stop a mortal heart.

Even in New York, humans apparently expect shops to keep something approximating regular business hours, so now that I have the shop to look after, I've found all sorts of new uses for enchantments.

Including a teeny-tiny probably-not-that-serious stimulant spell addiction.

I slurp down the rest of my spiked drink and give it time to fully work while I do my makeup for the day.

By the time I make it downstairs to unlock the front door of the shop, I'm fully awake and ready to face the world.

***

It only takes about forty minutes of me checking over the account books for me to give up. "Greta, you're a bitch," I mumble, watching the red ink turn into a blur before my eyes.

Not only has she kept her accounts in an archaic little ledger book, but she foisted them on me without a single job interview first.

What happened to what's mine is mine, huh? Like proper witches? Whoever heard of witches just giving their shit away?

But now I'm stuck with this damn place, and if I look at this stupid ledger for two more minutes, I'm liable to use it for kindling next time I need to start a fire.

I'd hire an accountant, but even I can read the ledger well enough to know that I can't afford it.

In short, Greta left me a pile of shit I didn't even ask for.

The bell over the door chimes, and I don't have to look up to know who it is. Violet always carries with them a distinct mystical signature.

With a witch father and a demon mother, Violet's magic is a complicated web I don't pretend to understand. It has a certain zing to it I've never felt with anyone else.

"One of these days you'll actually have to buy something," I tell them, stashing the ledger away so I don't have to think about it anymore.

"One of these days you'll have to start paying me," Violet shoots back.

"Yeah, good luck with that," I mutter. I can barely afford to pay myself at the rate things are going.

Violet asks most days. And every day I tell them no. But Violet turns up anyway, always re-organizing the crystal collection, despite the fact that it's rarely been disturbed from how they left it the day before.

Violet always has a pattern in mind, it seems, and I've given up trying to understand. Maybe it's just another product of their strange magic.

I turn back around at the counter, surveying the shop to see that Violet is, sure enough, at the crystals. "Love the top," Violet says, focused on their task.

I look down at myself. It's perhaps a bit daring, but probably not anything someone wouldn't expect of a magic shop proprietor in New York. People like the witchy look, even if the humans think it's a character.

And besides, if you have something worth showing off, you might as well.

"Wanna borrow it?"

Violet looks down at their own thin frame. "Know an enchantment to shrink it?" They ask wryly.

I do, actually, but the bustier fits me perfectly right now and there's no way in hell I'd mess with that.

Violet just turns to their daily task of re-arranging my crystals. "You're not, like, cursing the shop with those, are you?" I ask.

"I didn't enchant these."

Not necessarily a no, then. But probably a no.

So I leave Violet to their daily strange task and turn towards the enchantments in the back.

Most everything Greta kept in the front of her shop would pass muster if a human wandered in. They do, sometimes. This is New York and they're every-where. They wander in to purchase a crystal or a candle or an orb or something they think is a good luck charm. Most of them aren't even enchanted, although Greta had the habit of enchanting the odd one with minor little spells. No harm in bringing the occasional human a little extra luck.

But the real stuff, we keep in the back. Greta is—was—the rare witch who could actually build relationships among other witches, and people came to her

224

from far and wide for enchantments they couldn't or wouldn't do themselves. She was able to convince all kinds to shop with her.

Now they come to me. I wonder if they still will when word gets out that Greta is gone, and it's just me here.

Not that I've made enemies. I'm friendly enough. Certainly friendlier than most witches. But I'm no Greta.

But Greta is gone. Apparently on some semi-permanent beach honeymoon with her secret beau, and she left no forwarding address. Just instructions on how to keep the shop open that look like she wrote them as an afterthought.

Sure, Greta. Just leave your life behind. I'm sure bottomless mimosas and sunny beach reads and sex in the waves forever are worth it.

I may be a little bitter.

I try to push it away. Bitterness won't pay the bills.

***

I'm working on enchanting scrying orbs when the bell over the door chimes again.

I don't stop. It's a difficult, finicky little enchantment that Greta taught me decades ago. Not everyone can do it, so I figure enchanting a host of the things will maybe be a money-maker for the shop.

I keep right on enchanting, humming the tone that goes into the orb as I pour energy into them, assuming the chime is just Violet leaving for the day.

Right up until I hear Violet's yelped, "Hey!" and feel a heavy presence intruding on my back room.

ALSO BY ADDISON JAMES

Crae Romance

Callum

Bryce

Heath

Celia

Silas

Estrid

Supernatural Christmas

A Werewolf for Christmas

A Recipe for Love

Standalones

The Heat Cure

Dragon's Treasure

ABOUT THE AUTHOR

Addison James is a romance book author from New England. They are obsessed with all things mythical, mystical, and magical. A lifelong fantasy reader, that evolved to fantasy romance as they grew up. Addison always has a story to tell and is excited to introduce you to their world of fantasy romance. Addison can be reached through Tiktok, Instagram, or Threads (@Addyjameswriter), through email at addyjames@addyjameswriter.com, or through their website, www.addy jameswriter.com.